The Primrose Heart

Lynn Story

To Larry, with all my heart.

There are nearly five hundred species of primroses with nearly an infinite number of hybrids and cultivars. Cultivated varieties usually carry the common name of primrose, and they generally share a similar shape—low rosettes of dark green leaves with umbrels of colorful flowers that arise on sturdy stalks in spring. There's a lot of variety in primrose flowers. Some varieties have clusters of flowers on a single stem, while other primulas have one flower per stem, with stems that create clusters of flowers that skim the rosette of leaves. They may remain evergreen in the zones where they are hardy. Primroses prefer temperatures of 50-60F degrees which makes very early spring and even March in Hampton Roads suitable for primroses depending on the variety. Four species of evening primrose are native to Virginia — three bloom at night and one during the day. The flowers are large with four petals.

Chapter One

It had been a long day at work and Sarah Nelson had visions of falling asleep on the sofa in her favorite pajamas, watching a movie. But clearly that would not happen. Someone was banging on her apartment door. She reluctantly got up and looked out to see who it was, her co-worker Rob again. She jerked open the door.

" You having to stop coming by here all the time, stop calling me and stop harassing me at work!"

"Sarah, can't we at least be friends? I promise I'll stop calling so much."

"I'm sorry Rob but, this is how it as to be!" She was shaking now, she wasn't sure if it was from anger or fear. "We can't because you can't move on. Stalking me when I'm out with friends and calling me at work is not acceptable."

"Sarah, you're being unreasonable!"

"No, I'm not. It's been a year, Rob. You have to forget about me!"

"I can't forget about you! You're such a wonderful person, so kind...."

"Stop it! Stop it!" Sarah was so angry she didn't notice the cold of the night air or even the police car that had pulled up.

But Rob noticed. "You called the police?" He screamed.

"No, I didn't."

"You bitch!"

Sarah gasped at Rob's language. "Rob, it wasn't me!"

"Sir, step over here for a moment," one of the officers instructed.

The second officer steered Sarah back into her apartment. "I'm Officer Manning. Can you tell me what is happening here tonight?"

"Rob and I dated very briefly. It wasn't really a relationship. We only went out three times, and that ended a year ago." Sarah peeked over Officer Manning's shoulder out the open door to see what was happening outside. "He follows me, he calls me, I've told him to stop, but he always says he wants to be friends."

"Ma'am, you may want to file a restraining order for your own protection. Without one, there is little we can do when he comes back, but ask him to leave."

"I don't know," she chewed her thumbnail, "I never thought Rob could be violent until tonight. Tonight, he is a completely different person."

"Ma'am, these things have a way of escalating. I have the forms right here on my tablet you can complete right now. No taking off from work." Office Manning pointed to the tablet she was holding, trying to reassure Sarah.

Sarah glanced at the door again. The look on Rob's face made the decision easy.

"Okay, I'll do it."

Officer Manning tapped on her tablet and brought up the necessary form. "Use this to check the appropriate boxes." She handed Sarah the stylus.

"Sarah!" Rob yelled from outside.

Sarah jumped.

"Don't worry about him. He isn't going to bother you anymore tonight. After we submit the restraining order, if he bothers you again, you just all us and we can arrest him."

The words were meant to be comforting; they were anything but. Sarah's hand shook.

Officer Manning nodded her approval as Sarah signed the form with the stylus.

"I'll print a copy in my patrol car for him. Lock your door after we leave and keep it locked. If he comes back, call us."

She handed Sarah her business card. The front had the officer's contact information and on the back was a crisis hotline number. Rob was still yelling. He had seemed like a nice, quiet man when they had met at work. His shy demeanor was attractive. He didn't like going out or being around other people, and their dates involved sitting at home and watching old movies. Sarah tried to break it off gently. The problem was he didn't take rejection well, and he seemed to be obsessed with her. Her friends had tried to warn her, telling her he was weird and a loner. She thought he was just socially awkward, and people were judging him unfairly.

After the police left, Sarah sank down in a chair and pulled out her phone to text Jennifer, her friend from work, to let her know what had happened and to ask if she might come over and stay the night. Sarah was shaken, and while she was sure Rob wouldn't be back tonight, she didn't want to be alone.

"Eryn, are you ready?"

"Yes," Eryn Upton stepped out of her office to meet her friend Penelope affectionally known as Penn.

Penn appraised Eryn's clothes. "You're going dressed like that?"

"Of course, I'm a horticulturist, not a banker. I don't wear suits to work every day."

"I realize that, but you could change out of your garden clogs."

"Oh! I knew I was too comfortable." Eryn kicked the clogs off under her desk and quickly slipped on more suitable footwear. "How's this?" She asked, modeling her leather boat shoes.

Penn made a face. "Only marginally better."

Eryn laughed as she turned off the lights and followed Penn out to her car for the community meeting being hosted by the Gates Point Chamber of Commerce and the West End Business Association. Tonight, the new Chief of Police was going to address the business community's concerns over the recent vandalism and threats that had plagued many of the businesses in the west end.

The community room was nearly full by the time Eryn and Penn arrived. They slipped in and took seats in the back of the room.

Eryn looked around at the crowd. "Looks like a good turnout."

Penn frowned. "Just means these people are potential victims, just like us. I'm glad people are taking a stand."

"Look, there is the president of the Chamber of Commerce." Eryn pointed out.

Penn followed Eryn's gaze. "Who's that man in the expensive suit?"

Eryn studied the man; she couldn't tell if the suit was expensive or not, but she did appreciate the way the mystery man filled it out. "How do you know it's expensive?"

"I'm in fashion design. I know the difference between an off the rack suit and a tailored suit."

Penn was whispering something else, but Eryn had been too interested in Mr. Expensive Suit to hear what she had said. "Huh?"

"I said, I hope we actually get to voice our concerns."

"Oh yeah, me too." Eryn nodded.

A moment later, the Chamber President stepped up to the podium.

"Good evening everyone, and thank you for coming out tonight." She looked around the room and smiled. "Can you folks in the back row hear me well enough?" Penn and Eryn, along with several others, nodded in the affirmative. "Great, then I don't think we need the microphone for tonight." She continued with her introduction, "Many of us have had the misfortune to have either been vandalized or had items shop lifted. Chief Keegan is here tonight to talk about the Police Department's role in combating this latest crime wave and how we can all work together."

There was a small round of applause as the man in the tailored suit walked to the front of the room. Eryn was immediately struck by the color of his eyes. The rest of the room melted away and all Eryn could see was dark hair shorn close on the sides, with an errant curl dropping over Chief Keegan's forehead as he spoke. His pale blue eyes were a striking contrast to his dark hair.

"Good Evening and thank you all for inviting me here tonight. I hope this will be the start of a new relationship between the west end business community and the police department."

"Boy, he is a smooth talker." Penn whispered.

"Yes," Eryn agreed absently.

She watched as he scanned the room, making eye contact with different members of the collected group. Finally, his eyes met hers and she suddenly felt very uncomfortable. She gave him a small smile, hoping he would turn his attention elsewhere quickly, instead he held her gaze long enough for the heat to rise in her cheeks.

Several minutes later, as the speech was winding up, Eryn considered how she might slip out of the meeting unnoticed. She suddenly felt very self-conscious about her appearance as she sat there in jeans, a company sweatshirt, and boat shoes with no socks. By contrast, Penn was wearing an elegant drop shouldered dress of her own design with leggings, boots and a high collar leather vest. She wasn't sure why she cared what this man thought about her. She looked around the room and her blue jeans didn't seem completely out of place. Some people were dressed in suits, jeans, khakis and everything in between. Nearly everyone had some sort of sweater or light jacket since January could be a little unpredictable. It had been in the fifties earlier, but the night promised to be cold.

"There are displays and refreshments in the next room and I look forward to talking to each of you one on one." The Chief smiled and several people approached him.

"Ready?" Penn asked.

"Yes!"

Penn looked at Eryn, who was never a fan of crowds but seemed to be in more of a hurry than usual to leave. "What did you think?"

"It was okay, I guess." Eryn hedged. She knew if Penn found out how Chief Keegan made her feel, Penn would never let her live it down. "He didn't really tell us anything we didn't already know." Eryn added.

"What's gotten into you tonight? You're usually more of an optimist than me."

"I'm sorry. I think maybe I'm just tired."

Which was true. Running her own landscaping and nursery business, Eryn worked fourteen-hour days on a regular basis and never took any time off.

"Come on, let's go. I'll take you out to dinner and you'll feel better." Penn offered.

"Sounds good to me." Grateful Penn wasn't putting up a fuss about staying and meeting the police chief. Eryn headed for the door.

They had almost made it out when Penn paused to look at a map displaying the various crimes the west end had experienced recently. It was unnerving to see it displayed that way. The west end was an older but well cared for part of the city. It had turned a little more artsy in recent years, but that was okay. The more coffee shops and bistros, to go along with newly established indie art galleries and craft shops meant more business for them all.

"Good evening." A voice said from behind.

Eryn felt her heart sinking.

"Well, hello." Penn flashed her super model smile as she turned to face the Police Chief. "Can you tell me how current these figures are?" She pointed to the map, pretending to be interested. Eryn rolled her eyes as visions of escaping the meeting were dashed.

"They are current as of two days ago when I was putting this together. I wanted to get the most recent data." Chief Keegan smiled back.

"I see." Penn turned back to the map and tapped a cherry red nail against the legend of the map. "This is the response time, but what is the time frame for apprehending the suspects?"

She could tell Penn was quite proud of herself for watching all those police dramas on TV.

"That's an excellent question. He smiled and looked over at Eryn briefly.

"It depends. If the business has cameras and caught anything, we can use that will help us in tracking down the suspects. The time is often much quicker."

"I see. I wonder if I should upgrade my security." She was flirting in full force.

"I could have one of our community liaison officers come by and evaluate your system." He offered.

The look on Penn's face made Eryn want to laugh out loud. She was clearly disappointed the Chief hadn't offered to come by himself.

Chief Keegan then turned his attention to Eryn. "Do you have a business here as well?"

Eryn had to swallow a giggle before she could answer him. "Yes, I own Sandcastle Nursery."

"I know that place. I bought some trees for my yard there and my gardening supplies."

Penn looked furious and surprised all at the same time. "Oh, does your wife enjoy gardening? Penn interjected.

Eryn was ready to strangle her on the spot but decided committing murder in the presence of the police chief probably wasn't the smartest plan.

"No, I'm not married." The chief answered her while he was still looking at Eryn.

"Excuse me, Chief?" Mr. Zimmerman from Mr. Z's market approached, drawing Chief Keegan away.

"It was a pleasure to meet you." Eryn said to the Chief as she grabbed Penn's arm and began dragging her towards the door.

"Ouch! okay, okay. What's the hurry?"

"I'm just not in the mood for crowds tonight."

"You'll feel better after you have something to eat." Penn repeated her earlier offer.

"No, can you just drop me by my place? I'm exhausted."

"Okay, sure." Penn gave her a look of disappointment.

Eryn's guilt kicked in, "I'm sorry, we can have a girls' night this weekend."

Once, home with her shoes off and a glass of wine in hand, Eryn leaned back and thought about those pale blue eyes. She shook her head. She needed to forget them. Men had only proved to be trouble for her.

The weekend had gone too quickly after the drama with Rob on Friday night. And normally she wasn't excited for Monday morning, but this morning Sarah was up early and ready to start her new job. Sarah had interviewed with Eryn Upton at Sandcastle Nursery just a couple of weeks ago, and Eryn had called her back the next day to offer her the job. It was tempting to start right of way, but it was only fair for her to give her current boss two weeks' notice. She was excited about the change and the challenge. The pay was a little better and there were benefits. Sarah had never worked in a nursery before, but the atmosphere seemed more relaxed and less 'corporate'. The dress code was certainly more casual. She could wear jeans if she wanted to, although she opted for a dress her first day. This seemed like a dream come true. Eryn was pretty laid back, considering she ran her own business. All the other employees worked in the greenhouses or out in the field doing installation and maintenance. It would just be Sarah, Eryn and a couple of part-time employees in the retail building, which was also where the office was located. And most importantly, no Rob coming down from the IT department to chat with her or stalk her in the employee cafeteria.

The January morning was chilly, but the sun was shining. Sarah felt good about her new start. She took a moment to appreciate the world around her. The commute was easy, and she didn't even mind when someone cut her off in traffic. She parked in the gravel parking lot and took a deep breath before walking inside.

"Good morning Sarah, and welcome aboard." Eryn greeted her.

"Thank you."

"Why don't we get you settled in the office and then I will take you on a tour and introduce you to everyone?"

"That would be great."

Eryn led the way to a small but tidy office. "The office is a little bare, but you are welcome to decorate it anyway you like."

"This is great." Sarah looked around and thought about the possibilities.

"Here is the key to the office door and the desk. Feel free to use them as you see fit."

Sarah pocketed the keys after dropping her purse into the bottom desk draw.

"Ready?"

"Yes, ma'am."

"The next office over is me." Eryn pointed; Sarah peeked inside. It was decorated in warm colors and soft lighting. It wasn't much bigger than her own office. "Over here is the kitchen."

Sarah made note of a full-size refrigerator, coffeemaker, toaster, and a microwave. She was in the habit of bringing her lunch.

Next, they went out to the retail shop and Eryn introduced Sarah to Bethany, who worked part time, and then out to the greenhouses to see the heart of the operation and meet a few more people. Most of the employees were part time and worked on different days. Installation was done on Mondays, Wednesday's and Fridays. Maintenance was done on Tuesdays and Thursdays for both residential and commercial properties and commercial projects only on Saturdays. It was easy to see why Eryn needed help with the financials.

"Eryn, I know it will take me a little time to get up to speed, but I want you to know I want to help you and take some of the weight off your shoulders. This is a lot to deal with every day."

Eryn smiled and relaxed her shoulders a little. "I look forward to that."

Chapter Two

Rob sat watching Sarah's apartment. He was angry when she refused to even talk to him on Friday, and then she signed that restraining order. But, after he had time to think about it, he realized it probably forced her to sign the order by the police. That is why they had kept them separated. Still, he wanted to respect her wishes and give her some space. So, he parked a block down the street and just kept an eye on things to make sure she was okay. He still didn't understand why she didn't love him the way he loved her, but he hoped that by giving her some space, she would come to realize just how much they needed each other and how much he could do for her. He would treat her like a queen and take care of her. She would never have to work, and she could stay at home with their children and be happy. Sarah hadn't gone out on Sunday, but today she left early wearing a beautiful dress he had not seen before. She must be going to work, so he followed her to make sure she got there safely. But she wasn't going in the right direction. Rob wondered if she was sick and going to a doctor's appointment or something. He changed lanes and tried to keep up with her but lost her in traffic. He decided he would have to try again tomorrow.

Tuesday, he followed Sarah again. This time, he could keep up with her in traffic and noticed that she had a new job. Why hadn't she mentioned this on Friday when he was at her apartment? Rob decided he needed to check this place out and make sure this was the kind of place Sarah should spend her time. He slowed as she pulled into the parking lot, but he had to keep moving and made a mental note of the business name. When he got to work, he would look them up online.

He spent an hour carefully studying the website for Sandcastle Nursery. They listed a few of the employees with a brief biography and a list of their areas of expertise with landscaping and plants. He jotted down their names so he could investigate each one to make sure they did not pose a threat to Sarah. After work, he took the route that would allow him to drive past the nursery on the way home. He made a plan to leave work early later in the week so he could sit in the parking lot of the pharmacy across the street and make notes of the employees as they came and went. He might be able to learn something valuable. Sarah was so careless that he couldn't believe it. Shee working with criminals and not even know it. But then she wasn't an IT person, so she probably didn't know how to research people to find out if it was safe. It was another reason why she needed him.

Matt, the greenhouse supervisor, head into the office, "Eryn, the pump in greenhouse three is on the fritz again."

"Great!" Eryn stood up and stretched. She had been training Sarah on the business and the bookkeeping, and while a break was welcome, this wasn't what she had in mind.

"Sarah, I'll check back with you later."

"Go ahead, I'll be fine. I'm sure I have enough information to get me started."

Matt led the way to the greenhouse.

"Have you checked all the connections?"

"Yes, ma'am. It seems to not be getting enough power."

Eryn stopped to pick up the toolbox on the way.

"Well, I've been nursing this system in greenhouse three for a while. I knew it wouldn't last forever."

"I'm afraid we might be there." Matt said, standing aside so she could look at the pump.

"Can you grab a couple of people and start watering the plants with the hoses? We might have to do it this way for a few days if I can't get this thing running again."

"Sure thing."

Matt strode away to recruit some help.

The automatic irrigation system in the greenhouse was the oldest had apparently finally gave out. After inspecting the pump, Eryn headed back to the office to place an order for the needed part. As she passed through the retail shop, she noticed a man looking at the rain gauges.

"Have you been helped yet?" she asked, approaching him from behind.

The man turned around; Eryn was staring right into those incredible blue eyes of the police chief.

"Yes, I have thanked you..."

"Good afternoon, Chief."

"Good afternoon."

Why did he have to smile like that? The kind of smile that reached his eyes and looked genuine, she thought. She chased the thoughts away, "You said someone was helping you?"

"Yes, a young man is scheduling a spring delivery for me."

"It's smart to schedule ahead, we book up quickly."

"Yes, I made the mistake of waiting too late last year. He chuckled.

"Are you one of our regulars?" She was hoping her voice wasn't giving her away. Her voice always sounded an octave too high when she was nervous.

"Well, I've only moved to Gates Point last year, so I'm probably not considered a regular yet."

"Oh." That explained why she didn't remember seeing him in here before.

He looked around briefly.

"You have a very efficient staff; the few other times I've been in I've always been treated very well."

"Good I'm very glad to hear it."

"Mr. Keegan?" Brad approached. "You're all set."

The chief turned to Brad. "Thank you very much."

Brad nodded and then looked at Eryn. "Eryn, Kelly called while you were in the green house, and she won't be in today."

"What next?" This day was just going from bad to worse. "Okay, thank you. Brad. Can you go help Matt in greenhouse number three, the pump is broken, and we need to water everything with the hoses."

"Yes, ma'am."

Brad jogged off in the direction of the greenhouse.

"Bad day?"

She breath out a heavy sigh and put her hands on her hips, "It isn't one of my better ones."

"Why don't I buy you dinner tonight, help you forget about it for a while."

Eryn was stunned. It had been a long time since anyone had asked her out to dinner.

"Thanks, but I'm afraid it is a little early in the day for me to be making dinner plans. I will likely not leave here at a reasonable dinner hour." She felt the heat rising in her cheeks at the thought of having dinner with this man. The idea of having those piercing blue eyes staring at her across a dinner table made her cheeks blush and her heart race.

"You still have to eat, and it doesn't have to be fancy. How about tacos and a beer and I'll bring you back here if that is what you want so you can finish up," he waved his arm around, "whatever needs finishing up." He smiled a charming smile that left no room for argument.

She could see she wasn't going to get out of this very easily. "Okay, sure." Her heart was pounding so hard as the words left her lips she wondered if the Chief could hear it.

"Great, I'll text you later and we can decide on a time."

"That would be fine." She walked over to the counter by the register and grabbed a business card and wrote her cell number on the back. "Here you go."

He looked at it and smiled. "See you later." He tapped the card before placing it in his pocket.

Eryn hurried to the office breathing harder than she should be. What had she just done? She hadn't dated a man in years. She didn't have time for the complication of a relationship and with the Police Chief, no less. She needed her head examined. She took a deep breath, she decided if he called later she would just politely decline. Claim she was too busy or something. It would be easier to say no over the phone.

"Is everything okay?" Sarah asked when Eryn stopped at her doorway "You look pale."

"Well, I need to order a pump relay switch, so not as bad as it could be, I guess."

"If it helps I completed the reconciliation." Sarah smiled.

"Really?"

"Yeah, would you mind looking it over to make sure I didn't miss anything?"

"Sure." Eryn logged onto her computer and pulled up the files Sarah had been working on. She had done an excellent job. What a relief it was going to be to have her help me with the financial stuff. Now she could spend more time doing other things like avoiding the Chief Keegan and his incredible blue eyes. But, he did say he shopped here regularly, so how was she going to avoid him completely? Maybe she could just sell the business and mobe to Tathiti or something. She needed advice on how to handle the situation, the problem was, Penn was her best friend and the one with more experience dating, but there was no way she would ever tell Penn. She knew what Penn would say anyway, she would tell her to stop being such a bore and go out with the man, it couldn't hurt. But, Sarah knew from past experience it could hurt very much.

Chapter Three

Everyone had gone home, and all the doors to the nursery were locked. Eryn finally found a moment to log onto the supplier's website and order the part to get the pump working again. She had spent the afternoon moving plants into other greenhouses so that the manual watering wouldn't be as difficult. She couldn't afford to lose any plants from the inventory. Luckily, this time of year, the greenhouses weren't quite as full as they normally were, so she was grateful for that.

The cell phone in her pocket buzzed. She didn't recognize the number, but then read the message.

"Is now a good time?"

She had forgotten all about the police chief.

"Sure."

"What's your favorite taco?"

"Any kind is fine, really."

"Even fish tacos?"

"Love fish tacos."

"Be there in twenty minutes."

Butterflies in her stomach reminded her that she looked like a complete mess. She didn't have too many options. She didn't have a change of clothes with her, so a quick trip to the bathroom for to wash off as much dirt as she could and maybe try to drag a brush through her hair.

She stared at herself in the mirror. Why was she doing this? Hadn't she just told herself the night of the community meeting that she didn't need a date or a relationship? Eryn didn't have time for the complications that came with men. She had a business to run, and the business was going pretty well, a broken pump notwithstanding. She had just hired someone to help her with the paperwork for the first time. Why did she feel the need to complicate her life just when it seems like it was finally working out?

Exactly twenty minutes later, there was a knock on the glass door up front.

"Hi," Eryn said, opening the door. "You have your hands full. Let me help you with that."

"I've got it. Just point me in the right direction."

"Follow me." She relocked the door and led him to the back room. Her stomach rumbled at the smell of the tacos.

Once he had sat everything down on the dinette table, she realized the room felt tiny and closed in.

"I'll be right back." She said and dashed out to the retail area.

She grabbed a tablecloth and some accent pillows and went over to the patio table displays. Then went back to the kitchen and gathered up some utensils and plates.

"Anything I can do to help?"

"Sure, you can bring the food." She smiled. She led the way out into the display area where she had dressed up a patio set for their dinner. "I thought this might be more comfortable."

"This is very nice."

The string lights added a nice glow. They sat down and Chief Keegan began serving the tacos.

"I forgot cups."

"Do we need them?"

He produced a bottle opener from his key chain and set a bottle of beer down in front of her.

She was very curious about his behavior. Most men, especially men that looked like models, were not interested in woman who spent their days digging around in the garden with compost and plants.

"These smell so good. I don't think I realized how hungry I was." She tried to smile and maintain some semblance of table manners.

"Don't you eat during the day?"

"When I remember." She picked up a taco and took a bite not able to resist the food any longer.

"I understand. I do that too." He smiled and took a bite of his own taco.

"So, chief, what do they call you when you're not on duty? Or are you always on duty?"

He looked like he was going to choke. "I'm so sorry, my given name is Jeremy,"

He held out his hand across the table. She shook it and tried to ignore the electric shock wave that seemed to go straight to her heart.

"My friends call me Blue." He continued.

"Blue, that is an interesting nickname." She didn't want to state the obvious as ask if it was because of his eyes.

"Yeah, nicknames have a way of sticking if you don't want them." He chuckled.

She wasn't sure if that mean he didn't like the nickname and so she still felt like I didn't know what to call him.

"You mentioned you moved here a year ago. Where did you live before?"

"I moved down from D.C. when Chief Corey retired."

"I don't think I ever met him."

"Really?"

"Yeah, I don't really pay too much attention to local politics beyond the chamber of commerce. No offense."

"None taken." He sat back for a minute. "I guess everyone just has a different definition of community policing." He didn't believe in policing from behind the desk, not even for the chief.

Eryn smiled. She like his definition. Eryn helped herself to a second taco. She was starving and there was going to be none of that pretense of not being hungry or any of that other nonsense Penn would advise her to do when having dinner with a man.

"Have you always been a police officer?"

"No, I was in the military and then an NCIS agent before being offered a job with the DC police."

"Did you like it up there?"

"In D.C.?" He raised his eyebrows at her.

"Yes,"

"Not really."

She didn't ask him to elaborate. She could imagine that D.C. was a tough place to work especially for a police officer.

"What did you do for NCIS?"

"Pretty much what any police officer does. Investigate crimes. The difference was those crimes were specific to navy and marine personnel, families and property."

"Did you enjoy that?"

"Yes, I did, but I was getting tired of moving around. I did that in the military and then for NCIS, so I thought it would be nice to settle down somewhere."

"And you've picked Gates Point to settle down?"

He gave her a small smile. "Yes."

She nodded and munched her taco and then sipped the beer.

"What about you?" He asked.

"Oh, nothing as exciting as all of that." She laughed.

"Are you from Gates Point?"

"Yes."

"Have you ever lived anywhere else?"

"I went away to college when I was eighteen, like most kids. I suppose all I wanted to do was get out of here. So Penn and I applied to every college that wasn't anywhere close to home." She laughed at the memory. We had so many plans to take on the world back then.

"Penn?"

"Oh, my friend who was with me at the community meeting."

He frowned for a moment, like he was trying to picture her, and she had to giggle to herself. It would be highly offend Penn that she hadn't made more of an impression on him.

"So, where did you go to school?"

"the University of California at Davis."

"Wow, that's pretty far from here."

"Yeah, that was the plan."

"Then what?"

"Well, I graduated, and I wasn't ready to settle down to a job just yet and I love the water,"

"Hard not to if you're from here, I would imagine."

She nodded. "So, I spent a couple of years traveling around. I started with California since I was there already, then onto Hawaii and Australia."

"Wow, that sounds like a real adventure."

"It was, it was great. We lived in apartments, in tents on the beach, you name it."

"What did you do for money? Were your parents supportive?"

Eryn laughed out loud.

"There were pretty much anything but supportive. I shouldn't say that they didn't shun me or anything, but they had a hard time understanding why I didn't want to get an actual job and get into the rat race."

"Parents are like that." He picked up another taco and smiled a very charming smile.

"Penn and I taught diving lessons, took tourist scuba diving in Hawaii, I won a few surfing competitions. Penn was a bartender for a while."

She had to laugh at the look on his face.

"No really," she reassured him, "she wasn't quite so fussy back then. But we needed little money. We rarely had to pay rent. We just needed money for food and enough money to get to the next place on our itinerary."

"That sounds pretty outstanding."

"It was for a while, but like everything, it gets old, too. And so, I came home and started working in an engineering and planning firm, then at the local university, and then started my own business." Eryn paused and looked at him. "And that is probably more than you ever wanted to know." She suddenly felt embarrassed for having prattled on for so long.

He smiled an appreciative smile. "On the contrary."

She felt a little uncomfortable under the weight of his gaze. He finally broke eye contact, "Come on help me finish these tacos." He opened the box.

There were two tacos remaining and, and each grabbed one.

❧❧❧❧❧❧   ❦❦❦❦❦❦

Sarah left work late. It had been a crazy day. They had been shorthanded in the retail store, so she helped out as much as she could while Eryn had to deal with broken equipment in the greenhouse. She was exhausted and hungry, but she felt pretty good, too. As she unlocked the door to her apartment, she had a strange feeling that she was being watched. She thought about Rob and hurried inside and double locked the door. Then she made sure all the windows were locked and the curtains closed. Suddenly, she felt very exposed. She decided she was just being paranoid, and it would not let it ruin my plans for the evening, which was to put on some fuzzy socks and make homemade Mac and cheese for dinner.

Rob watched as Sarah come home late from work and rushed into her apartment. He saw the light come on and imagined her kicking off her shoes and relaxing on the couch. This new job was already working her too hard; she was coming home late. He worried she wasn't eating properly and taking care of herself. He smiled, thinking about what it would be like when we were married, and she wouldn't have to work. They would go on picnics on the weekends and maybe have children one day. Sarah would be an excellent mother. She just needed to realize how much he loved her, and then she would understand that they needed to be together. He needed to find another way to make her understand that they were meant to be together, and this new job wasn't helping. He punched the steering wheel and vowed to find a way to show Sarah how much he loved her.

❧❧❧❧❧❧   ❦❦❦❦❦❦

"Penn, it's seven o'clock in the morning. What are you doing up so early?" Eryn held her cell phone between my shoulder and her ear while she fixed a cup of coffee.

"I've been worried about you. You have answered none of my texts since yesterday afternoon."

"Well, I'm sorry, mother, but I've been a little busy."

"Don't get sarcastic with me!" Penn was on a roll this morning and she wasn't letting Eryn off the hook.

"I was busy. Yesterday was the day from hell. The pump relay switch went out in greenhouse three. We had to water everything by hand that couldn't be moved into another green; I had two people called in sick, plus I'm training a new bookkeeper and I really just didn't have the time to read text messages."

"Okay, well, I'll just pretend that I know what you just said."

"Penn, you are such a girly girl."

"Thank you. "

Eryn was glad Penn couldn't see the eye roll.

"Well, I'm very disappointed." Penn continued, undeterred.

"Why?" Eryn was hoping Penn hadn't found out about her private dinner with the police chief.

"Well, I thought you were ignoring me because you had a hot date."

Eryn sighed. "Well, I had a date last night with a man, if you must know." Eryn chided herself as soon as the words were spoken.

"What?"

"It was a sort of late-night picnic. But listen, I've got to get an early start this morning. I'll call you later and tell you all about it. Bye!" She hung up laughing because she could just imagine the look on Penn's face.

Eryn drove to work, thinking about the previous evening with Blue. They had talked for hours, and it felt like she had known him all her life already. It was as if they had become best friends over night. But, on the other hand, he seemed like a complicated man, and she wanted to know more and yet she kept asking herself, why? Why did she feel compelled to even think about a relationship?

Eryn was the first to arrive at work and was just booting up her computer when the employees' only entrance door slam shut.

"Eryn, where are you? Show yourself right now!"

"I'm in here, Penn!" She should have known Penn wouldn't wait for her to call. The joy of taunting her was short-lived.

Penn appeared in the doorway with a baseball cap, yoga pants, an oversized t-shirt and pink slippers. Eryn nearly spit coffee on her desk.

"Oh, my god!" Eryn exclaimed, more in shock than from humor. Penn never left her house without being dressed to the nines and yet here she stood with no make-up on in her slippers. If Eryn hadn't known better, she would have thought someone had died.

"How dare you hang up on me!"

"Penn, are you okay?" Eryn was biting her cheek to keep from laughing.

"No, I'm not okay. I mean, what is this world coming to when my best friend in the multiverse doesn't call me the minute she gets home from a date to tell me about it?"

"You didn't give me a chance."

"What do you mean, I didn't give you a chance? When did you get home?"

"About six this morning, barely enough time to shower and change."

"Oh, wow!" Penn sunk into a guest chair.

"So, you see you didn't have to come all the way over here wearing," Eryn paused for dramatic effect. "Whatever that is."

Penn looked down at herself.

"Oh god!" she screeched.

"It's nice to see the real you again." Eryn smiled.

Penn laughed. "Well, here I am in all my freckled face glory."

"I like your freckles. I think they're cute."

Penn rolled her eyes. "Are you going to tell me about this date or not?"

"Not. I want to savor it for a while before sharing."

Penn's expression softened. "I can understand that."

"Thank you."

"Will you at least tell me his name? I mean, I broke about ten traffic laws getting over here."

"Okay, I guess I can tell you that much. His name is Blue."

"Blue? What kind of name is Blue?"

"Sorry, that is all you get."

"Blue? Okay, fine. God, I need to get home before anyone sees me."

"And she's back." Eryn laughed, standing up to hug her.

"I'll call you." She wagged her finger at Eryn and headed for the door.

It had been a long time since Blue pulled an all-nighter. He should have been tired, but spending time with Eryn only served to energize him. The thought of her would get him through the day more than any amount of caffeine.

He had a full day ahead of him, meetings with the station chiefs, the city manager, and a news reporter about the most recent homicide. Blue sent her a quick text before the madness started, thanking her for a wonderful evening and suggesting they do it again soon. When he didn't get an immediate response, he wasn't concerned. Blue hoped she was getting a little sleep, but he had a feeling that she was probably back at work.

Chapter Four

"Morning!" Sarah called as she came through the door.

"Morning." Eryn forced a smile as Sarah bounced into the office.

"Oh wow!"

She stopped at Eryn's door.

"I look like hell, don't I?" Eryn knew she must. It had been years since she had stayed up all night.

"You just look a little tired. Did you even go home?"

"Just long enough to shower and change."

"Why don't you go home for a few hours. I'll call you if anything major happens."

Eryn smiled. It was tempting and she had no doubt that Sarah could handle the day to day, but she had never called out and she wasn't about to start now.

"I appreciate it, but I have so much to do today."

"Do you want to borrow a little concealer?"

"Concealer?"

"Yeah, it could lessen the dark circles under your eyes."

"I don't wear make-up normally; I wouldn't know how to put it on."

"No worries, I'll take care of it." Sarah smiled digging into her bag and producing a little tube.

"You know I'll probably just sweat all of this off, right?"

"It's waterproof." So, you won't."

"Then how do you get it off?"

"Wow, you really don't wear make-up, do you?"

"No,"

"I'll get you some make-up remover at lunch,"

"Sarah, thanks."

"For what?"

"This."

"Don't be silly, sisters have to look out for one another."

Eryn smiled up at her as she finished.

"There you go, looks perfectly natural. So, you'll be perfect in case you see the reason you were up all night."

Eryn looked up at her in surprise.

Sarah laughed. "Girl, the only thing that ever keeps a woman up all night is a man." Sarah laughed as she returned the beauty supplies back to her purse.

It was later in the day when Penn came bustling into the shop like a human hurricane.

"Hello, may I help you?" Sarah greeted her.

"Oh hello," Penn glanced at Sarah mentally making a note of her size and stature. It was a habit of being a designer. "I am looking for Eryn."

"She's in one of the green houses, I can page her for you."

"Thank you."

Sarah sent a text to Eryn letting her know a customer was requesting to speak with her.

"Would you like anything while you wait?"

"No thank you." Penn started circling Sarah. "Have you ever thought about modeling?"

"What?" No!" Sarah was stunned by the question.

Penn continued to study her. "You would be perfect, what's your style?"

"My what?"

"Penn leave her alone." Eryn said entering the shop. "Did you have Sarah page me?"

"Yes, I did."

Sarah was trying to slip into the background confused and uncomfortable with Penn's assessment of her and now she was worried she had done something wrong by paging Eryn.

"I've been texting you all morning." Penn crossed her arms.

"And I have been busy."

"Yes, I can see that." Penn stared at the dirt on Eryn's hands and clothes. "But I thought you'd like to have lunch."

"Sorry Penn, no time."

"Okay, but I'm desperate for a girl's night out, can you have dinner tonight?"

"I guess so." Eryn agreed against her better judgement.

"Wonderful!" Penn turned to Sarah "And what about you sweetie? Are you available for dinner tonight?"

Sarah looked surprised and stared at Penn and then at Eryn.

"Me?"

Penn nodded to her.

"Um, yes I'm available."

"Great!" Penn fished out her cell phone and handed it to Sarah. "Add your number to my contacts and I'll text you both later with the details."

Sarah tentatively took the phone and entered her information.

"Okay, have to run!" Penn waved as she floated back out the door.

"Wow!" Sarah said after Penn left.

"You said it. I swear I think she is getting worse as we get older."

"Have you known her long?"

"We are old friends." Eryn watched Penn as she pulled out of the parking lot in her white Mercedes.

Sarah watched as well, but with quite a bit more envy than Eryn. "She is very glamorous."

"Yeah, she reinvented herself after college. She spent a couple of years in Milan studying fashion design and came back like that."

"Milan, really?"

Oh yeah. You'd never know she is the daughter of a tugboat captain and grew up on the docks. But don't tell her I told you that."

Sarah looked at her surprised and then giggled. "You're right I would never have guessed that in a million years."

⁓⁓⁓⁓⁓⁓   ⁓⁓⁓⁓⁓⁓

Are you ladies ready?" Penn called out letting herself into Eryn's house.

"We are."

"Okay, let's go!" Penn turned on her heel and headed back out the door.

Sarah slid into the back seat of a very expensive Mercedes. The leather seats were soft and supple, and she sunk back into them.

"Where are we headed?" Eryn asked slipping into the front passenger seat.

"There's a dinner party at the country club to kick off the weeklong golf tournament. I got us all tickets." Penn smiled as she pulled away from the curb.

"Is it formal?" Sarah asked suddenly panicked that she was underdressed.

"No, sweetie it's not black tie, you'll be fine." Penn smiled in the review mirror.

"The country club really? You know I hate that pretentious stuff." Eryn huffed.

"I know, it won't be that bad and besides I need a wing woman or two."

When they arrived, Sarah was able to relax a bit, as the attire was indeed varied and not a black tie in site.

Eryn stepped up next to Sarah.

"I'm sorry about this, I had no idea."

Sarah smiled taking in the people and the formal surroundings of the club. Never had she imagined she would ever see the inside of the country club.

"It's okay, I think it will be fun."

Eryn rolled her eyes.

Once inside Penn stopped a passing waiter and snagged champagne for herself and Sarah, knowing Eryn wouldn't drink it.

Eryn could see Sarah was enthralled and Penn had a protege in the making. She slowly melted away from her two friends and retreated to the edge of the crowd. The country club wasn't really her style she was more of a Chamber of Commerce Fish Fry, sort of social butterfly. The people here, while local business owners were in a different league. But she did enjoy people watching and there would be plenty of opportunity for that this evening.

Eryn slowly made her way to a set of French doors open to the evening air passing by a couple arguing over where to put the new outdoor hot tub, oh to have such problems, she thought. She slipped out onto the terrace to find a bar and more revelers. She sighed at the thought it was going to be a long night.

"Yes, ma'am what can I get for you?"

"Are you serving anything other than champagne?"

"Yes, ma'am..."

"I believe the lady would like a white wine."

A voice sounded from behind her.

Eryn turned to see Blue standing behind her grinning from ear to ear.

"Unless, of course, you need something stronger."

"Wine will be fine." A smile forming on her full lips.

"And for you, sir?"

"Club soda."

The bartender served their drinks.

"Shall we?" Blue pointed in the direction of a bench near one of the outdoor heaters and away from the crowd that would afford them a little privacy.

"I had no idea you golfed." Eryn said.

"Only when I have to."

"Are you a member here?"

"No," Blue laughed. "Not even a police chief makes that kind of money."

The January air was just chilly enough that Eryn was grateful she had thought bring a wrap with her and adjusted it around her shoulders.

"What about you?" Blue asked, "what brings you out to the club?"

"Penn." Eryn sighed.

"I'm sorry?"

"My friend Penn, that I told you about last night?"

"Right, and where is your friend now?"

"God only knows. This was billed as a girl's night out and we ended up here. Penn knows I hate this sort of thing."

"Penn doesn't have a date?"

"Apparently not, and if she was seeing someone, she wouldn't bring them here and ruin her chance of finding something better."

"Sounds like a lonely person."

"Commitment isn't really her thing and whatever her thing is, it seems to be working for her."

"And she ditched you already?" Blue had a protective tone in his voice. She liked it.

"No, I ditched her, if she had her way, she would be parading me past every eligible bachelor in town." Eryn nearly bit her lip and then recovered. "Besides she has Sarah with her tonight."

"Sarah, the young lady that works for you?"

"Yes,

"Seems like a nice girl."

"She is."

"Did you get any sleep this morning?" He wondered if she was as tired as she was.

Eryn blushed a little, "No, I went home after you left and showered then went back to work."

"Do you ever take a day off?"

"Rarely, too much to do when you run your own business."

"You need more help."

"More help costs money."

"But you did recently hire Sarah?"

"She is my office manager and bookkeeper. She helps out in the retail shop, too."

"I can't imagine having to deal with that daily. I spend way too much time in budget meetings, and I have a whole department to handle that for me."

Eryn laughed. "Yes, well the police departments quite a bit larger than my little landscaping business."

They sat just enjoying each other's company for a few moments.

Blue finally broke the silence.

"Do you want to go somewhere and get a bite to eat?"

"Sure." She felt her cheeks heat up. "Let me just text the girls to let them know I'm leaving."

She pulled her phone from her purse.

"Leaving with a friend, see you later."

"Okay." Was the simple reply from Sarah.

"With a male friend?" Penn text back.

Eryn sighed and ignored the text.

They waited for the valet to bring Blue's car around.

"What are you in in the mood for?" Blue asked.

"Honestly? I am famished I could go for anything."

"Okay, well any food allergies?"

"No, no allergies."

"Great! I know just the place then."

The car arrived and Blue helped her then bent down to look at her.

"Excuse me, while I make a phone call."

"Certainly."

He stood up and closed the door. She could hear the muffled sounds of the conversation.

"Chuck? Blue here, you still open tonight?"

"Hey Blue, yeah I'm open. Are you stopping by?"

"A friend and I are looking for a place for dinner and I was telling her what a good cook you are."

"Her?"

"Yes, her."

"Anything for a friend." Chuck laughed.

"Okay see you in ten." Blue ended the call and slid behind the wheel. "All set?" He asked.

"Yes." Eryn nodded.

Blue drove to the marina which boasted several restaurants in the area plus a couple of very nice hotels. Blue drove to the end of the wharf road to a restaurant that was accessible by both car and boat. The sign read The Seabreeze. The parking lot only had a handful of cars it and Blue parked close to the building and under a light.

They were greeted at the door by a large man with a buzz cut and dressed as a chef.

"Blue, you old bast. . .I mean, son of a gun."

"Chuck, I'd like you to meet a friend of mine, Eryn."

Chuck gave her a warm smile and held out his hand. "Hi Eryn."

"Hello." Eryn smiled shaking his hand. She instantly liked Chuck. He had warm brown eyes and a gentle grip despite his hand being rough and the size of a bear paw.

"Come on in, I have a spot for you."

Chuck turned and led the way.

Blue let Eryn follow behind Chuck. She liked the feeling of his hand resting lightly in the small of her back.

The spot turned out to be in a cozy table in an empty dining room, with a candle lit in the center.

Blue raised an eyebrow at Chuck.

"The candle too much?"

"No, it's perfect." Eryn answered.

He nodded to her, winked at Blue before disappearing.

A moment later a server appeared to take their drink order.

After they had sipped their ice teas. Eryn looked out the window at the lights on the water.

"This is lovely."

"I'm glad you like it."

Chuck appeared at the table. "Does the lady enjoy seafood?"

"Yes, I love seafood, does the chef have a recommendation?"

Blue watched the banter between the two of them and smiled. He had known Chuck for what seemed like a lifetime. And Chuck was a hard man to impress.

"I recommend the crab, always, but tonight we have a seafood boil. However, if you prefer something less 'hands-on' I would recommend either the stuffed flounder or the seafood casserole."

"The seafood casserole sounds delicious."

Chuck turned to Blue. "And for you?"

"The stuffed flounder."

"Very good."

Chuck disappeared again and Blue hoped they would have a few moments alone.

Blue drank a more tea, his throat was dry for some reason he felt nervous and didn't know what to say. Somehow the impromptu taco dinner had been less nerve wracking than this. Finally, he blurted, "Tell me a little more about you." He said for a lack of anything else to say.

"I'm afraid you already know everything there is to know about me."

"I seriously doubt that."

"I hate to disappoint you but I'm really very boring."

"Again, I doubt that, but let me see, so far I know you're from Gates Point, you left and went to college, then traveled around the world surfing and now you're a workaholic with a best friend who is definitely not."

"That is me in a nutshell. What about you?"

"Well, you know I am currently the police chief of Gates Point."

"Yes, I gathered as much." Eryn played along with is little game.

"Before that, I was an NCIS agent."

"Yes, you did mention that briefly."

"I did?"

"Yes, but you didn't tell me if it was NCIS or the police department that taught you how to evade questions so well." Eryn gave him a wicked smile.

"Well, I would assume I learned it in the same place you did, college."

"Oh yes, well that is the whole first year of the landscape architecture program." She laughed.

He loved the way she laughed.

"Touché" Blue began to relax a little more.

Their food arrived via one of the waitstaff.

Blue was relieved that Chuck hadn't brought it out himself, he could be a charmer and Blue didn't like the idea of competition with Eryn.

"Seriously, why do you avoid talking about yourself and relationships?" Blue narrowed his gaze at her.

"Probably because they never seem to work out well for me." She said softly.

He saw the pain in her face and regretted his question.

"I'm sorry."

"No need."

She brightened instantly. It was clearly a pain she was used to dealing with.

"Well, I'd be happy to meet that guy that caused you this pain and pound his face in if that would make you happy."

Eryn gave him a smile and shook her head no.

"I mean it you just say the word."

"He passed away."

"I'm so sorry, I didn't mean. . ."

"It's okay. Don't worry about it.

Chuck's voice interrupted the moment.

"Eryn you'll have to excuse my friend here he has a very special gift of saying exactly the wrong thing at the wrong time."

Eryn was embarrassed that Chuck had overheard their conversation.

"Oh, I wouldn't go so far as all of that." She defended Blue.

"Blue, you need to hang on to this one, she defends you even when you put your foot in it."

"Don't you have something burning in the kitchen?" Blue growled.

"Yes, your dessert."

Chuck gave Eryn a wink and left.

"Your friend is quite a guy."

"He thinks so." Blue took a bite of his fish.

"Have you known Chuck long?"

"Too long."

"Did you work together at NCIS?"

"No, I've known him longer than that."

"Really?"

"We were in the Marine Corps together."

"Really?"

Eryn was finding out there was more to Blue than met the eye.

"Was he a cook in the Corps?"

"No."

She sensed he wasn't interested in discussing that part of his life tonight. She didn't want to push.

After they had finished their meal, Chuck presented them with a chocolate soufflé.

"Oh, that looks too good to eat."

"Talk like that will put me out of business, young lady."

"Would you like to join us?" Eryn offered.

Chuck laughed as he pulled up a chair much to Blue's chagrin. "Boring you to death, already, is he?"

"Tell me Eryn, how did you meet my buddy here?"

"Oh, at a community meeting where he gave a very moving presentation."

Blue raised an eyebrow at her.

"Really?" Chuck looked from Eryn to Blue. "A moving presentation?" He laughed a deep laugh. "I suspect the moving part was the audience fleeing the room."

Eryn laughed.

"Shut up, Chuck." Blue grumbled and he tried not to laugh himself.

"More rapier wit?" Chuck teased.

Blue was visibly miserable, and Eryn felt sorry for him.

"And how many awkward dates have you had since that fateful encounter?"

Blue looked like he wanted to punch Chuck.

Eryn stared at Blue while she answered Chuck's question. "We have had a couple of lovely dinner dates and Blue is always a gentleman and very charming."

Chuck nodded. "Well, I can tell you this, he is sincere. If he tells you something you can believe it. He isn't going to waste time on bullsh...fluff."

Eryn ducked her eyes and then looked up at Blue.

"I know." Her voice was a whisper.

Blue nodded and hoped his five o'clock shadow was hiding the redness of his face.

She sensed how uncomfortable Blue was, so she tried to change the subject.

"Tell me what Blue was like back when you first met." Blue looked like he was ready for this date to end.

Chuck grinned; he was enjoying this more than he should. "He was about as socially awkward as he is now. But I will admit that he did save my butt on more than one occasion."

"Interesting," Eryn was intrigued and sat with her chin resting in the palm of her hand ready to hear more.

"Eryn," Blue interrupted, "I forgot to mention the Chuck here is a serial liar."

She rolled her eyes at Blue.

Chuck leaned in conspiratorially.

"Did he tell you how he got the nickname, Blue?"

"No."

"Chuck, she doesn't want to hear that story."

"Yes, I do."

"Okay well during World War I there was a group of French soldiers call the Diablo Bleus and they were known for wearing blue capes and having great courage in battle."

"So, he got the nickname because he is very courageous?" Eryn smiled with pride.

"Not at all, he wore this ridiculous blue cape everywhere he went." Chuck howled with laughter.

Eryn couldn't help herself and she laughed too. After a moment Blue joined them.

"I'd better be getting Eryn home."

"Okay, Eryn it was a pleasure meeting you, come back anytime." Chuck stood and shook her hand.

"Thank you, the food was amazing."

"Blue, good to see you, my man."

They hugged and slapped each other on the back.

"Thanks. You, too. Now what do I owe you for dinner?"

"It's on the house." Chuck waved him off.

"No, it isn't."

"Hey, I don't take orders from you anymore, buddy. If I say it is on the house, then it's on the house."

"Okay, fine." Blue held up his hands in mock surrender.

"You're keeping the lady waiting."

"See you next week." Blue said as he turned to leave.

"What's next week?" Eryn asked.

"We have a unit reunion, and this year Chuck is hosting it."

"Do all of your unit members live in Gates Point?"

"No, we are scattered all over the world, but we have an annual reunion with as many of us as we can."

"That's wonderful." She squeezed his hand, "If you like I can prepare centerpieces for the tables."

Blue stopped halfway to the car and looked at her.

"That is really thoughtful."

She smiled. "I'd love to do it. Just tell me how many you need.

"Can I get back to you on that?"

"Of course."

They arrived at her house and Blue insisted on walking her to the door.

"Would you like to come in?"

"No, I'd better not. We'd probably stay up all night talking, and I know you have an early start in the morning."

Eryn smiled relieved that he understood, but also a little disappointed.

"Okay, talk to you tomorrow?"

"That's a promise." He reassured her.

He knew he should be walking back to his car by now. But he couldn't leave.

Eryn knew she should open the door and go inside but she just couldn't make her body move in that direction.

Blue stepped closer and cupped Eryn's face with both hands. He waited to see if she protested but she didn't.

He leaned down and hesitated once more before gently kissing her. Her lips were soft like rose petals and warm. He had the strongest urge to kiss her more passionately, but he feared that would only send her fleeing. He pulled back and looked down into her eyes.

"I need to go." He said, his voice a husky whisper.

Eryn didn't speak. She couldn't speak. She was afraid she'd ask him to stay.

She nodded slightly.

"I'll call you tomorrow."

"Okay. She managed to squeak out.

Chapter Five

Rob watched as Sarah stumbled out of the cab and up to her apartment. His blood was boiling. Where had she been all night? She was out partying while he sat waiting for her to come home. Didn't she know he was worried about her? She must have new friends at her new job that were making her act this way. His Sarah wouldn't go out partying and come home drunk. Rob needed to fix this. He started the car and slammed it into gear. He didn't care if anyone heard his tires squealing. Sarah was in danger, and he needed to save her. Arriving at the nursery, Rob parked on the street, away from the lights in the parking lot. He hurried up to the side of the building. There were some large rocks in the flower bed. He picked up several and threw them through the windows. He kicked out the remaining glass of the window and began overturning shelves and displays in the retail shop. There were sirens in the distance. He ran back to his car. When he got home, he was still breathless from the excitement. He couldn't settle down and he paced around the living room.

"That will teach them!" He shouted to the empty room. Maybe now Sarah would start to realize how much he loved her and how much he wanted just to care for her. He would treat her like a queen.

Eryn could see the damage as soon as she pulled into the parking lot. She had only been asleep an hour when the security company called to alert her to the break in. The lights from the police cars cast an eerie glow over the scene. She stepped through the door that was propped open, escorted by a police officer. She turned on the lights and gasped.

"Damn!"

"Ma'am, can you check to see if anything like money was stolen?"

"Of course." She went to the office and looked to see if they had tampered anything there with, then she checked the small safe.

"Nothing else looks out of place." She informed the officer.

"Do you know anyone that might have done this, a disgruntled employee?"

"I have had to let a couple of people go recently. But I can't imagine they would do this."

"You never know." The officered looked tired.

"I'll get you a list of names and contact information."

"Thank you."

After the police left. Eryn began cleaning up the mess.

About an hour later, employees arrived, all asking what happened and how they could help.

Soon all the glass was cleaned up, the displays were right and damaged merchandise separated from the stuff that could still be sold.

Sarah walked in. "What in the world happened?"

Eryn looked up happy to see a friend.

"You should have seen it a couple of hours ago."

"What can I do?"

"Can you make a sign to let people know we're still open?"

"Sure."

"Then keep an eye on things out here. I need to go call the insurance company."

"Of course." Sarah nodded.

Sarah began collecting letters to change the message board out by the road.

The other employees finished up in the shop and headed to their regular duties, all shaking their heads about the damage to the store.

As soon as Eryn hung up her desk phone with the insurance company, her cell phone rang.

"Hello?"

"Eryn, it's Blue."

"Hey." She sunk back in her chair, the sound of his voice comforting.

"Is everything okay?"

"No, someone broke into the store last night. They broke out all the windows and wrecked of bunch of stuff in the shop."

"Are you alright? You weren't there, were you?"

"No, I was at home asleep."

"Did you report it?"

"I have an alarm system and the security company called me and the police. There was a report made and I just hung up with the insurance company."

"Do you need me to come over?"

"Yes, but I know you're busy and we can talk tonight if you're available."

"Okay, if you're sure."

"I'm sure. I'll be fine. There is a lot of paperwork to do for the insurance company.

"I'm glad you weren't there when it happened."

"Me too."

"Call you later?"

"Okay."

Eryn clicked off and slid the phone back in her pocket. She needed some fresh air and to check on things up front.

"Eryn." Sarah called out to her.

When Eryn reached the front of the store, there was a young woman wearing khakis and a polo shirt with a glass company logo on it, standing next to Sarah.

"Hi, I'm Megan with Shine Thru glass. Your insurance company called us."

"That was fast."

"Well, we try to get out right away when it is a business client. We know you need to be secure in your business." The young girl said, smiling while she held a tablet.

"Okay, great, when can you start?" Eryn asked. This was all moving so fast, she had barely enough time to process what had happened and now she was already in repair and move on mode.

"Well, first, I'll take a look around and get some measurements for the estimate back to the insurance company."

"Okay, well, let me know if we can do anything to help." Eryn gave her a tight smile.

Megan nodded and turned to get to work, then paused.

"Do you have a security system?"

"Yes, there were sensors on the doors and windows."

"Okay, I'll work up an estimate for windows with embedded sensors and the external sensors."

Eryn nodded. She had a feeling she already knew the answer to that question. She could not afford the embedded sensors.

Another car pulled into the parking lot, this one with the security company emblazoned on the door.

"Why don't you let me handle this one?" Sarah offered.

"No, I appreciate it. I'd better handle it." Eryn patted Sarah on the arm. She took a deep breath, then stepped outside. It was going to be a long day.

At noon, Penn arrived with a small army of other business owners from the west end neighborhood with lunch for all the employees.

"Penn, you didn't have to do all of this." The outpouring of support was overwhelming.

"We have to stick together."

"This is exactly the kind of thing we were talking about at that community meeting. I certainly hope the police are going to do something." Penn was genuinely upset.

"Well, there were certainly enough of them here when I arrived this morning, and I'm sure they are working on it."

"Well, I have half a mind to call that police chief and remind him of the promises he made."

"I'm sure he has enough on his plate at the moment."

"Well, this better be one of them."

Eryn hugged Penn. "Thank you so much for this."

Penn smiled. "Don't think this will get you out of telling me who you left with last night, either."

Eryn couldn't help but giggle just a little. "I was afraid of that. No sympathy at all, huh?"

"None." Penn hugged her again.

Eryn smiled. She knew she would have to tell her eventually.

"Excuse me, Eryn." Sarah interrupted.

"Hi Sarah, how are you today?" Penn asked.

"Oh, I'm fine."

"Ah, youth." Penn rolled her eyes.

"Eryn, the police chief is here to see you."

"Perfect!" Penn pushed past Sarah and Eryn.

Eryn ran after her. "Penn!"

But Penn was already standing in front of Blue. "Chief, so good of you to come and make good on the promises you made at our community meeting." Penn smiled sweetly.

Blue looked around. It was obvious he wasn't expecting to see a crowd.

Eryn stopped short and made a sympathetic face over Penn's shoulder.

Blue was trapped as other members of the community realized he was there.

Eryn was determined to try to rescue him.

"Chief, so good of you to come by. Would you like something to eat? Then we could chat in my office if you like."

"No, no thank you. I just heard about the damage and wanted to stop by personally."

"That is so kind."

But Penn was having none of it.

"So, what is the department doing about this? Do you have a suspect yet?"

"We are looking at several people of interest."

"That is code for you have no idea."

"Penn!" Eryn interrupted. "I'm sure they are doing everything they can. It's only been a few hours."

Blue sensing, he would not be able to talk to Eryn privately decided that perhaps he should get back to work. "Ms. Upton, please let me know if you need anything."

"Thank you."

Blue spoke to a few more business owners that were still milling about and left.

She stepped into her office for a moment to send him a text apologizing.

Finally, everyone had left, and the shop looked almost normal again except for the boarded-up windows.

It was only Sarah, Penn, and Eryn left in the store.

"Well, I have a splitting headache. I think I am going to call it a day." Eryn said, rubbing her temples.

"You should go home and get some rest." Sarah felt bad for Eryn. She could see that she was used to shouldering her burdens alone, and she wanted to help. "Why don't you take the morning off tomorrow? I'll handle the shop and if anything really weird comes up, I'll call."

"You do look like you could use some sleep." Penn agreed.

"I'll think about it." Eryn stood up. "Thank you both, y. You wonderful friends."

Sarah and Penn followed her outside and waved as she pulled out of the parking lot.

Penn turned to Sarah, "Well, my dear, it's just us. What do you want to do this evening?"

"I don't know. What you had in mind?" Sarah asked.

Penn smiled, eager to have someone with enough energy to stay out all night with her.

"Well, first let's go shopping."

"I have a pretty tight budget in that department."

"Don't worry, we'll go shopping at my store."

"Oh, okay." But Sarah had a feeling that would not help the budget situation at all. She was pretty sure anything in Penn shop could blow her wardrobe budget for a year.

Rob sat in front of Sarah's apartment building fuming for the second night. He had been interrupted when sending his message this morning. And clearly it had not been enough to send Sarah running back to him. It was past time for her to be home from work and she was hours late. Where could she be? She wasn't at the nursery he had driven by there on his way here and her car was gone. And he couldn't see inside because of the plywood that had replaced the windows he had broken. Maybe he needed to send a clearer signal. He began to wonder if she was with another man.

No! She wouldn't do that to him. But the seed of doubt was planted, and he needed to know. How would he find her? He needed more information. He wanted to leave and go home and do research, but he had to know that she got home safely.

Sarah spent the evening with Penn, they ordered pizza and had it delivered to the Penn's Boutique. Penn had a wonderful eye for style and was happy to help Sarah pick out a few pieces to build her wardrobe. She was more than understanding about Sarah's budget.

"I tell you what we can do. I have a fashion show coming up and I need some models, if you would be willing to help me out, I'll let you keep the pieces you model or exchange them for something more your style."

"Oh Penn, that is way too generous. I mean I would enjoy modeling; I think. I've never done anything like that before."

"Listen," Penn lowered her voice. "I was where you are now once. And I know what it is like, I do. This isn't charity, this the barter system. I don't need money. You need to keep what money you have. But I need a fresh face to model some of these clothes and you need some clothes. So, it is a win/win situation."

"Okay, I guess that sounds fair."

"Unless you plan to be a bookkeeper forever."

"No, I suppose not."

"If you like what you do and you want to keep doing it there is no harm in that. The world needs bookkeepers. But nothing says you can't have a little more if that is what you want."

"Yeah, you're right." Sarah smiled.

Penn put a few things in a bag and handed it to Sarah,

"This should get you started."

Sarah hugged her before accepting the bag. "Thank you, Penn."

"Just make sure you tell everyone where you got the outfit when they tell you how fabulous you look."

"I will!"

Sarah was almost crying tears of joy when she left the shop and headed home. She couldn't wait to see what Penn had put in the bag for her.

As she opened the door to her apartment, she heard a car start down the street. The sound was not unusual, there was a mix of apartments and single family houses up and down the block, but something about the sound caught her attention. She looked around to see if she could see which car had started but she didn't see anything suspicious. She shook off the feeling and went inside.

Rob drove home with the intention of finding a better way to protect Sarah.

Chapter Six

In the days that followed Eryn was consumed with getting her shop repaired and making the center pieces for the reunion at Chuck's restaurant. She was loading up the van to deliver them when her phone buzzed with a text message from Blue.

"Wish I could see you."

She responded, "me, too"

He had been busy with work and coordinating the annual reunion with his former marine unit.

She added, "I'm heading to Chuck's now."

"Be careful, he believes that he is charming and might try to woo you away from me."

"Not a chance." She laughed as she returned the phone to her pocket and climbed in the van.

The restaurant was in chaos or so it seemed. She walked through the front door and looked around. A young woman stepped over.

"Can I help you?"

"I'm with Sandcastle Nursery I have your center pieces."

"Oh great, just bring them in here and we will sort them out for the tables."

"Okay."

Eryn turned to see Chuck.

"Eryn?"

"Hi Chuck."

"What are you doing here?"

"Didn't Blue tell you? I made the centerpieces for the tables."

"He must have left out that detail." Chuck walked out to the van with her. "I'll help you carry them in."

"Thank you, but I can manage."

"Don't be silly."

She opened the back door to the van.

"Wow, I don't know a lot about plants, but these are beautiful."

"Thank you. The flowers are primroses." She appreciated his honest opinion.

They each grabbed a box and carried them inside.

She and Chuck spent a few minutes arranging them on the tables.

Chuck looked around the room at how the centerpieces improved the tables. "Do you grow those flowers in your greenhouse? He asked looking over at Eryn.

"I did grow them, but primroses will bloom in winter, they don't mind the cold as long as it remains above freezing." She beamed up at him proud of your work.

"How much do I owe you?" Chuck asked when they were done.

She gave him a knowing smile. "It's on the house."

He laughed at her echoing his own words back at him. "I don't think so, not for this."

"Yes."

"Hey, why don't you join us?"

"No, it's a guy thing, you don't need me hanging around."

"Well, Sunday, spouses, families and significant others are invited, are you coming with Blue on Sunday?"

She looked at him and blushed.

"No, I have a ton of work to do."

"On a Sunday?"

"Well, my shop was broken into earlier this week, and I still have a lot to do."

"I hadn't heard about that, I'm really sorry is there anything I can do to help?"

"No, the insurance is getting the repairs sorted pretty quickly, it just all the paperwork and the investigation."

"With all of that you still made these arrangements?"

"Well, I told Blue I would."

"You really have to let me pay you."

"Nope," she waved her hand and headed for the door. "it's on the house. Like I said."

"Okay, thanks, Eryn." Chuck watched her leave.

As he watched her pulling out of the parking lot, he took out his cell phone and dialed Blue's number.

"Keegan."

"What is wrong with you?"

"Nice to hear from you Chuck."

"Yeah, I bet, listen Eryn just dropped off the center pieces."

"Yeah, she told me she would be stopping by the restaurant."

"And you didn't think to invite her to dinner on Sunday?"

"Well, no."

"Why not?"

"I don't know. Why, did you say something to her about it?"

"Well yeah, because I assumed you had mentioned it."

"What'd she say?"

"She was busy, you jackass. Because she was probably hurt that you hadn't asked her."

"Oh."

"Blue, my man, sometimes you are thicker than a plank."

"Look it's complicated."

"No, it's not. You like her, she likes you. You ask, if she says no, then okay. But you at least ask."

Chuck clicked off shaking his head.

Blue stared down at his phone. Chuck had a point. But he had wanted to keep Eryn to himself a little while longer. He had made an exception with Chuck and Eryn hadn't even told her best friend Penn they were dating. They were keeping things low key. But maybe he had made a misstep in not asking her. He would have to call her later and arrange to see her.

"Boss? You ready?" He looked up to see his assistance holding the door for him to head inside the conference room for yet another meeting.

"Yeah."

✺৵৵৵৵৵ ৳৳৳৳৳৳

Rob called in sick the next day. He needed time to work on this project. Sarah was much more important. It took him only an hour to assemble a tiny GPS tracker with a power source. Tonight, he would secure it carefully to her car. He would need to make sure that the antenna stayed parallel to the ground and that it was safe from the weather. He pulled up the specs for her car on the manufacture's website and then found an online repair manual so that he could determine the best location for the device. He carefully sealed it in a Ziplock bag to protect it from moisture.

His next project was to find a way to make sure no one was leading her astray or endangering her. He knew she had blocked him from social media. He needed to create a different online persona and try and friend her, maybe even pose as another woman. That would be perfect. He smiled to himself and began creating an online profile. He had seen a picture of her when he was at her apartment with her high school logo, so he found the high school online and looked for a name of someone that she might not have been friends with, but she might remember if she checked the yearbook. Once he was done, he went searching for her online. He sent her a friend request and waited.

He checked the time, he needed to go to the gym if he was going to keep to his daily schedule. He spent two hours at the gym working out and then picked up take out on the way home. He was anxious to see if she had responded to his request yet.

He poured a glass of sparkling water and logged on to his computer.

Yes! She had accepted the friend request now all he had to do was get her to trust his online profile enough to tell him what he wanted to know. He was patient. He could wait.

He started by uploading a post about his weekend plans which were just as fictional as his profile. A little while later Sarah sent a like and commented that she was looking forward to seeing the movie he listed as his weekend plans. He leaned back and smiled to himself. This was going to be easier than he had hoped.

He finished his take-out food and the water. He would sit here all night if he had to, to get Sarah to trust 'Emily' his online profile.

Eryn was sitting at home when she got a text from Penn.

"You up for a girl's night in?"

"Only if it involves pizza, beer and yoga pants."

"I'll be there in ten."

Eryn got up and grabbed plates and made sure she had enough beer. Twenty minutes later Penn knocked and came in.

"Sorry I'm late, I stopped for beer just in case you didn't have enough."

"You always think of everything!"

"I try." Penn followed Eryn into the kitchen.

"This smells wonderful."

"Tell me why you are home on a Saturday night?"

"Why are you?"

"Touché`." Penn answered.

They grabbed their plates and the beer and went to settle in on the sofa in the living room.

"Want a movie?" Eryn picked up the remote.

Penn settled back into the sofa, "Sure, what did you have in mind?"

"I don't know something with a lot of explosions."

"Okay," Eryn flipped through the channels and settled on a World War II action movie.

They ate their pizza and finished the first beers.

"Want some more?" Eryn asked pausing the movie.

"Yeah, sure."

They both went to the kitchen.

"Eryn, you want to tell me what is bothering you?"

"Nothing."

"Well, I know you better than that, and you know it."

"Something is bothering me, but it's petty and stupid and it shouldn't bother me and talking about it will only make me sound petty and stupid."

"Wow, all that?"

Eryn threw her a sour look.

"Does this have anything to do with the mystery guy you've been dating?"

"Maybe."

"Want to talk about it?"

"I do but I don't want to be judged." Eryn sat back down on the sofa.

"Whose judging?" Penn protested, "Okay, okay no judging."

"I've been dating this guy for a few weeks now."

"The guy named, Blue?"

Eryn was dreading this part; she took a sip of beer for courage and to stall.

"Yes."

Penn snorted then caught herself. "That is an interesting name."

"It's a nickname, his given name is Jeremy."

"Jeremy? As in Jeremy Keegan? As in the chief of police?" Penn was practically bouncing up and down in her seat.

"Yes." Eryn pointed a finger at her "You promised no judging."

"Whose judging? I'm just asking a question."

"Okay, fine."

"But can I make an observation?"

"I suppose."

"He is hot as hell!"

Eryn couldn't control the giggle that escaped her lips. "I know, he is, isn't he?"

Penn set her pizza down and leaned closer. "Tell me everything!"

"Okay, well after the community meeting, he stopped by the store to schedule a delivery for spring."

"That is months away!"

"I know so I was thinking maybe it was just a smoke screen."

"So, what happened?"

"He asked if I'd like to have dinner and I told him I was really busy with work."

Penn rolled her eyes.

"So, he brought tacos back to the nursery after closing and we sat at one of the patios displays and talked literally all night."

Penn squealed like a schoolgirl. "Are you serious? That is so romantic!"

"I thought so too, but I didn't want to read too much into it. But we've been texting every day."

"Is that who you left the party at the country club with the other night?"

"Yeah, I didn't know he was going to be there, and we just sort of bumped into each other.

"Oh! Do you think he knew you were going to be there and arranged to just 'bump into you'?"

"How would he have known; it was a last-minute thing with you."

Penn looked disappointed "True. So, then what happened?"

"We left there, and he took me to the restaurant down on the water called the Seabreeze,"

"I've been there, the food is really good."

"Blue is friends with Chuck the chef, they were in the military together. Anyway, his friend arranged a romantic booth and cooked us this special dinner."

"Wow, it is good to have friends in high places."

"Then Chuck joined us, and we sat and talked for a while." Eryn's tone changed and she looked back at the TV the images frozen.

"So, what happened?"

"Well, they are having some sort of unit reunion this weekend and I offered to make the center pieces for it."

"Okay," Penn was sensing Eryn was about to get to the point.

"When I delivered them to the restaurant Chuck invited me to stay, but I said no it was a unit thing. But then he said I should come back to brunch on Sunday when the family and spouses would be included."

"Okay, so what's the problem."

"Blue, didn't mention anything about the brunch on Sunday. And I can't very well just show up and crash the party."

"You wouldn't be crashing, Chuck invited you."

"That is not the point."

"Oh honey, maybe there is a good reason why he didn't ask you to go with him."

"Yeah, like I'm a hideous toad and only should be viewed under the cover of darkness!" She knew it was ridiculous, but Eryn started to cry.

"Oh my god! You know that is not true!"

"Well, I don't look like you or even Sarah which is apparently super model material."

"Oh no!" Penn hugged her best friend. "You are totally super model material, but you hate that sort of thing."

"I know I do, which makes me sound petty and stupid."

Penn couldn't help but laugh just a little. "No, it doesn't."

"You think I'm being stupid."

"No, I don't. Maybe a little over sensitive, but not stupid."

"You think so?"

"Yes, I think so. You know you are beautiful just the way you are. You can knock 'em dead with mulch on your shoes, dirt under your nails and straw in your hair." Penn laughed. Me, I have to primp, wax, curl, diet, and wear make-up and guys like Blue still choose you over me."

"You have lots of boyfriends."

"Sure, and none of them mean anything they are all superficial."

"You can change that Penn; you don't need expensive clothes and painted nails. You're beautiful under all of that."

Penn shrugged. "This is about you, not me."

Eryn wiped away a tear. "I'm stupid for getting upset."

"You're not stupid, men have a way of making us a total mess over things that make no sense. It is not your fault."

"You think so?"

"I know so."

"Thanks."

Penn picked up the beers and handed Eryn's back to her. "To us!"

"To us!"

"Now, let's finish this pizza before it gets cold."

Chapter Seven

"You call and invite Eryn to Sunday brunch after my pep talk?" Chuck had Blue in a corner of their annual unit reunion.

"Well, no."

"Why not?"

"Because I wasn't planning on coming, it's all about families and bounce houses and stuff."

"So?"

"So, you know I'm not into that and I never come."

"Well, I thought you might this year since you have Eryn."

"Well, I don't exactly 'have' Eryn."

"What does that mean?"

"It means we been dating but we aren't engaged or anything."

"So, you're not serious about her?"

"Of course, I'm serious about her! Why would you think I wasn't?"

"Well, you might want to give her a call."

"Why, what have you done?"

"Don't you remember, I told you over the phone I mentioned the brunch to her and asked if she was coming with you."

"You've got to be kidding me!" Blue pulled out his cell phone and dialed Eryn's number. "I didn't think you meant you actually said it like that!"

There was no answer. Blue shoved the phone back in his pocket and glared at Chuck, "Shit! What have you gotten me into!"

"Sorry man." Chuck walked away.

Blue tried texting Eryn.

"Need to talk to you when you have time. Call me any time after you get this."

Eryn heard her phone buzz in the other room, but she didn't feel like getting up to see who it was. She was sleepy from the pizza and four beers. Penn was already out cold from the food coma. Eryn curled up in the chair and pulled the afghan down over herself. Whatever it was or whoever it was could wait.

Eryn woke to knocking on the door.

She opened one eye and the light told her to keep the second one closed.

"Go Away!" Penn called.

The knocking continued.

Eryn uncurled herself from the chair and stretched. "Ow!"

"Be quiet." Penn muttered.

Eryn stumbled to the door and opened it. The sunlight was blinding.

"Wow!" Blue exclaimed.

She shielded her eyes from the sun and tried to focus, the voice was familiar but in her half sleep state she couldn't quite place it.

"Can I help you?"

"I doubt it." The voice chuckled.

"Who are you?"

The voiced laughed a little louder this time.

"Your savior, can I come in?"

"I guess." Eryn stepped aside still confused.

"Keep it down!" Penn shouted from the sofa.

Blue stood in the living room looking around. The TV was on pause, there were beer bottles covering the coffee table.

He guided Eryn to the chair she had obviously been sleeping in. "Sit."

Who was that?" Penn asked.

"I don't know." Eryn said pulling the afghan back around herself.

Blue shook his head and went straight for the kitchen,

He found the coffee and started a fresh pot, then cleared up the pizza box and the empty beer bottles.

It looked like Eryn and Penn had one hell of a girl's night and he hoped that the amount of beer consumed had nothing to do with what Chuck had told Eryn the night before about the reunion.

After the trash was taken out, he poured two small glasses of ginger ale found some bitters and added it, then took it into the living room.

Eryn drink this, it will make you feel better.

"No, it won't." She turned her head away.

"Yes, it will trust me."

She took it and drank. "Yuk!"

"Drink it."

"Fine."

She finished the glass.

Next, he went over to Penn.

"Drink this Penn."

"Go to hell!"

"Penn, drink this or I will force it down your throat!"

"Why?"

"Because I said so."

"Fine."

Penn never opened her eyes, she held out her hand and he put the glass in it. Then he held it steady while she drank it down in one.

"Good girl."

He took the glasses back to the kitchen and found mugs for coffee.

Eryn was starting to revive when he came back into the living room.

"Dear god! How did you get in here!"

"You let me in, and by the way you need to be more careful about opening your door before knowing who is on the other side."

Eryn shrunk under the afghan. "You can't see me like this!"

"Too late, and you're cute as a button." He kissed her nose and handed her coffee.

"Oh, I can't believe this is my life today." She sipped the coffee. "Penn! Wake up! A handsome man made you coffee!"

"What? Really?"

Penn sat up and stared at Blue.

"Oh my god!" She pulled the blanket over her head. "Are you freaking kidding me! No one sees me first thing in the morning."

Eryn laughed. "I do."

"That's different."

"Not today." Eryn laughed a little which made the pain in her head worsen.

"Well, at least he isn't my boyfriend." She peaked out from under the covers the smell of coffee too tempting. "I swear to god you better never speak of this to anyone." She said pointedly to him.

"Wouldn't dream of it."

Penn sipped her coffee. And sat up with a blanket firmly wrapped around herself.

"And you!" She said to Eryn.

"What did I do?"

"You sit there smiling in your yoga pants and morning hair in front of your boyfriend like it is the most natural thing in the world! No one should look that good with bed head!"

Eryn laughed. "Well, this wasn't my idea. But it's too late now and he hasn't run screaming from the house so how bad could it be?"

"Eggs with toast?" Blue called from the kitchen.

"He cooks too?" Penn asked incredulous.

"Apparently, so."

"You know this is incredibly unfair. And one of us is going to have to marry him."

"Why?"

"Because a man who has seen the two of us like this should not be allowed to walk around town with that knowledge unless he is attached to one of us. Otherwise, he has nothing to lose by telling people what we look like first thing in the morning."

"Why do you think anyone cares what we look like first thing the morning?"

"Well maybe not you, but I have a reputation."

"Yes, and there are many men in this town and the next that know what you look like first thing in the morning." Eryn laughed.

"You are unbelievable. When they see me first thing in the morning, I can tell you that it is very well orchestrated, and I assure you I look nothing like this! You just don't know who is taking your picture when you're asleep."

"Penn, you are something else. Why don't you sneak upstairs while Blue is making breakfast and fix your face? You can borrow something from my closet."

"Thank you, you're a true friend."

Penn sat the coffee down and dashed upstairs as fast as she could go without tripping over the blanket.

Eryn heard the bathroom door close and then a moment later a scream.

Blue raced in from the kitchen. "Is everything alright?"

Eryn sat smiling sipping her coffee. "Oh yes, that was just Penn looking at her face in the mirror and realizing you saw her with her make-up in shambles."

Blue looked down at Eryn and smiled sweetly. Then knelt down in front of her and brushed aside an errant strand of hair. "I need to talk to you about something."

"Okay." Eryn felt her stomach tighten.

"I saw Chuck last night and he told me he invited you to brunch today."

"He mentioned it."

"Well, he also mentioned to me that I should have mentioned it to you."

"Not if you didn't want to." She felt very uncomfortable and looked away.

"Eryn, I didn't mention it because I never go to the Sunday brunch at the reunion."

She turned back to stare at him.

"Why not?"

"Because it is for the families and it's all about bounce houses and face painting and stuff isn't my thing."

"Yes, but your friends will be there."

"Yes, and so will the children and the wives of the friends who didn't make it back and honestly, I still can't handle that."

She felt like an idiot for being hurt by his lack of invitation.

"Oh Blue, none of that was your fault. And I'm sure those families know it."

"You sound like Chuck."

She made a face at him. And he laughed.

She placed her hand on his cheek with a look of compassion. "Why don't you and I spend the day together here, I'll take a shower I promise."

He started to smile then jumped up.

"The toast!" He ran to the kitchen to pull two burnt pieces of bread from the toaster oven.

Eryn padded in behind him.

"Everything alright?"

"Well, we have charcoal if you want to cook out later." He held up the bread. "It was supposed to be cheese toast."

"How did you know I like cheese toast?"

"Just a hunch. I like it and I hoped you did too."

"Here let me help you with that. This thing is finicky, and you have to adjust it lower than you would normally for toast.

"Maybe you need a new one."

"This one still works; you just have to know how to work it." She shrugged.

He shook his head at her frugalness and her ability to be happy with what she had and to make it work for her. God, he was falling in love with her and didn't know if he should.

***

Rob sat in his apartment staring at the computer screen where was Sarah? She wasn't on any of her social media sites today. Tonight, he planned to install the tiny GPS tracker on her car. He planned to duct tape it to the frame near the control arm of her rear suspension. He hoped it wouldn't be noticed easily but he needed to be able to slide in and out from under the car quickly so as not to be noticed.

It was getting late, and he needed to shower and dress for church. He didn't want to miss mass this week. He hoped by the time he got back Sarah would be online. He knew she didn't go to church; he had asked her on their first date, and she said she hadn't been since she was a little girl. She would change her mind about that too, when he showed her all the wonderful things god could do for them and when she met Father Dave, he would help explain it to her as well. He smiled as he drove. He imagined them getting married in the church and Father Dave giving them his blessing. They would have children who would go to Sunday school and play with the children of the other young couples. They would be so happy together. She would see soon enough. He would make her understand. He entered the church and dipped his finger in the holy water before crossing himself, then slid into a pew near the front as he always did. He smiled and stared up at the large crucifix hanging above the alter. Soon. He promised the lord, he would bring Sarah here, soon.

Penn managed to make herself more presentable and rejoined Eryn and Blue in the kitchen.

"I have to say it is very nice of you to come over and cook breakfast for us, do you always break into your girlfriend's homes?"

"Penn!" Eryn hissed.

"I didn't break in, I knocked, and Eryn open the door."

"Penn, shut up." Eryn gave her a knowing look.

"It's okay, she is your best friend and I'm glad she is worried about you. Of course, not as worried as I was since I tried texting and calling since last night and I drove by the nursery, and you weren't there. I was afraid you might be ill or worse."

"So stalking is your thing?" Penn continued unabated.

"Penn, I swear to god if you don't shut up this might be the first murder committed in front of a police chief."

"Fine, fine, have it your way." She held up her hands.

Eryn put a plate down in front of her. "Here eat your stalker breakfast."

Blue hid a smile as Eryn slid the plate in front of Penn.

Penn didn't look happy, but she did look hungry, and she reluctantly picked up the fork and began eating. After she had finished, and Blue cleared away her plate she was more likable.

"That was delicious, you know you are welcome to stalk your way into my house and cook breakfast anytime." Penn cooed.

"Yeah, especially now that he knows what you look like with mascara rings around your eyes." Eryn dug in.

"Yes, well." Penn stood up, "That was a rare treat, one you will never see again. And I need to be going."

"Going where, church?" Eryn sniped.

"Shut up Eryn, you know I have inventory on Sundays."

"Hmm, mmm. Call me later."

"I don't know if I like your tone this morning." Penn huffed and left.

She could hear Eryn laughing as she closed the door behind her, knowing full well she would call Eryn later to find out how the day went with Blue.

"You were pretty tough on her." Blue said.

Eryn looked at him in surprise. "No, I wasn't. No tougher than she would have been on me and besides she knew I was joking. Trust me she will call me later to get all the juicy details."

He leaned close to her ear; it make her heart skip a beat. "And will there be juicy details to share?"

"I, uh, I don't know."

Blue chuckled. "Okay, maybe later." He sat down across from her. "What would you like to do today?"

"What?"

"Well, I'm here, and you seemed to be recovered from that wild pizza party last night, I thought maybe we could spend the day together, like you said earlier."

She hadn't expected him to take her so literally.

"Oh, well I don't know. What would you like to do?"

"What do you say we drive west on interstate 64 and see how many wineries we can visit in a day?"

"Are they even open on Sunday's?"

"I bet they are."

"Okay, sure. Let me go shower and change."

"Okay." He smiled.

Eryn stared at her closest for something to wear. What does one wear for a wine tour? Probably jeans and comfy shoes, check. She had those. What kind of top? She was over thinking this, she just needed to pick a shirt. It wasn't like she had a huge variety it was either a sweater or a button down. After, Blue having seen her in a t-shirt and yoga pants she opted for an oxford. He'd seen her rumpled now he could see her clean and pressed.

Blue stood up when he heard Eryn coming back down the stairs.

He watched and wondered how anyone could make jeans and a blouse look so good? He wanted to tell her he had changed his mind and they would be staying in the rest of the day just so he could look at her. But then he might sound like the guy Penn had been describing this morning.

Chapter Eight

Rob waited until ten that night. He watched as neighbors walked their dogs. He didn't want to take any chances of getting caught. He pulled the hood of his black sweatshirt up over his head. He stayed in the shadows until he got to Sarah's car then crouched low and ran as quickly as he could. He slithered beneath the car and placed the GPS tracker on the frame. Then removed the roll of duct tape from the pocket of his sweatshirt and wrapped it around the frame and the resealable sandwich bag. He was careful not to put any over the antenna so as to not interfere with the signal. When was done he slid out and slowly got to his knees and looked around, then stood and slipped back to the shadows?

Back in his car he opened his laptop and the software to see if the tracker was working. He waited and a minute later the unit showed up on the map. He could see the location of Sarah's car. He smiled and drove home, he no longer needed to risk sitting outside her apartment every night.

* * *

"Are you ready for the show tonight?" Eryn asked Penn over lunch.

"As ready as I'll ever be, I suppose."

Eryn turned to Sarah, "What about you?"

"I think I might be sick." Sarah looked as green as Eryn's salad.

"You'll both be great!"

"What if I trip and fall?" Sarah winced.

Penn looked as nervous as Sarah. "Oh god don't even say things like that."

"I don't understand you two. You've been working on this for weeks even months. Penn this isn't the first one you've done."

"I know but there are just so many things that could happen."

"Are any of those things within your control?"

"No."

"Then it doesn't do any good to worry about it. All you can do is to control the things you can."

"That is easy for you to say. You don't have to worry about the plants running amuck or anything."

"That's true, but I'm not going to apologize for choosing a profession where my product is more cooperative than yours."

Penn made a face. "Gee thanks."

"I'll be there, and I will help in any way should a crisis arrive." Eryn tried to reassure them both.

"Thank you, I know you will." Penn looked slightly reassured.

Eryn paid for lunch, and she went back to the nursery. She had given Sarah the day off to spend with Penn as they got ready for the fashion show tonight at the convention center. It was a big deal, not just the spring line of clothing but for brides planning their weddings as well, there where be hundreds of people there, not to mention vendors for miles. She was interested in visiting the vendor area, she had thought about expanding into areas she could provide plants on a rental basis for special events, especially weddings and she wanted to see what the competition might be and to get ideas.

Blue had also agreed to accompany her. She was working in the office when he text her.

"Looking forward to seeing you later."

"Same here."

They had been seeing more and more of each other and had seemed to have passed a milestone in their relationship. The winery weekend had been the turning point for her. They had spent the day driving from one winery to another, they ended it a little closer to home with a late-night picnic on the beach in the moon light. She would've been happy for that night to last forever. Blue's face in the moonlight so close to hers. The night had been perfect. The waves crashing on the sand couldn't compete with the sound of her heart racing when he kissed her.

She realized she wasn't the only one that had been kicked around by relationships. Tonight, he was going to meet her at the nursery and drive them both to the convention center. She checked the time and then pulled out the clothes she had brought to change into for the show.

She had chosen a blue dress with rhinestone trim and low heels and as she walked into the retail shop just in time to see the headlights of Blue's car sweep the parking lot.

He opened the door the shop and froze.

"Is everything okay?" Eryn asked.

"I, uh, yes." Blue closed the gap between them and took hands in his. "You are so beautiful."

Eryn felt the heat rising in her cheeks.

"Thank you."

He stared at her a minute more and then shook himself back to reality.

"Shall we?" He held his arm out for her. He waited until she locked the door and set the alarm.

They arrived a little early and visited some of the vendor stalls. He nodded to a few of the police officers working overtime to provide extra security. They saluted him and returned to their duties.

"That's pretty impressive."

"What?"

"Being saluted."

"You get used to it." He chuckled.

"Let's go check on Penn."

They walked to the back of the main hall, and she followed some people into the prep area.

She looked around for Penn for several minutes before she found her.

"Penn!" Eryn waved.

"Eryn!" Penn made her way through the crowd of women and men being pinned and tucked into their clothes.

"Wow! You look amazing! I should have hired you to model tonight."

"Not a chance."

"Blue, nice to see you. You two would be handsome on the runway together."

"Not me, but certainly Eryn."

"I didn't know you had any dresses like that." Penn admired Eryn.

Eryn smiled. "A girl has to have some secrets."

"Not from her best friend." Penn laughed.

"You are okay back here you need help with anything?"

"No, everything is under control. As much control as I can have over this chaos. Listen I have to run. You kids have fun."

Penn kissed Eryn on the cheek and disappeared into the crowd.

Eryn and Blue made their way back to the hall and found seats.

Penn's fashions were second on the program. They would be done early and then planned to go up to the rooftop restaurant for an after party.

❧❧❧❧❧❧ ❦❦❦❦❦❦

"I'm so nervous." Sarah whispered to the girl named Nikki standing next to her.

"Me too." Nikki reached over and squeezed Sarah's hand.

Then it was Sarah's turn, and she took a deep breath and tried to remember everything that Penn had taught her about walking with her chin up and doing the turn at the end without tripping over the hem of the dress.

She made it back safely and winked at Nikki as they passed each other.

Her next outfit was a much shorter skirt, so she wasn't worried about tripping this time. But when she got to the end of the runaway a face in the crowd caught her attend and she stopped mid-turn. Eryn knew something was wrong and looked in the direction Sarah was looking, but just as quickly as she had stopped Sarah was on the move again.

Eryn didn't see anything out of the ordinary. Just people watching the show.

"Is everything alright?" Blue asked.

"Yeah, I think so." She smiled and turned her attention back to the runway.

The master of ceremonies announced that was the conclusion of Penn's portion of the fashion show and gave information about where to find Penn's shop.

"I'm going to go backstage and check on Sarah and Penn, meet you up front in a mine?"

"Sure." Blue walked to the concourse as Eryn made her way to the backstage area.

"You all were amazing!" Eryn said to Penn and Sarah.

"Thank you. I'm kinda glad that is over with." Penn said looking a little less frazzled than earlier in the evening.

"Sarah, you, okay?" Eryn asked.

"Yeah, I'm fine. Hey, I didn't trip!" She smiled.

"Blue is waiting for us on the concourse to go upstairs to the after party."

"Okay, can you help me get this stuff out to the van and then we can go on up?" Penn asked.

"Sure."

Penn was the model of efficiency she had been packing up the clothes as they came off the models.

In only a short time they were up on the rooftop overlooking the city relaxing with a glass of champagne.

After an hour other designers joined the party and attracted Penn's attention. Eryn and Blue drifted to the other side of the rooftop.

They stood quietly admiring the skyline. Their view was to the north and the lights of the city provided a beautiful outline of the tall office buildings further uptown, the streetlights providing a lighted grid of the city. In the distance sirens could be heard.

"Does that bother you?" Eryn whispered.

"What?"

"The sound of the sirens when you're not at work?"

"No, not really. I always hope that whoever is answering the call will be safe and the person in need is reached in time. But if they need me, they will call." He tapped his pocket that held his cell phone.

She nodded and sent up a silent prayer for the officers to be safe.

"Have you ever been hurt in the line of duty?" Eryn asked.

He turned to face her and gave her a questioning look.

"I guess, I never really thought about it on such a personal level before." She explained.

"Yes." He said simply.

She felt a pang in her heart. She didn't ask for details and he didn't offer any.

"I don't want you to get hurt again." She said simply.

"Me either." He slid an arm around her.

"Mind if I join you?" Sarah asked.

They turned to see her standing a few feet away.

"Please do." Eryn reached out for Sarah's hand, "is everything alright?"

"Yeah, I guess I'm just not in the mood for crowds tonight."

"Sarah, are you sure? There was a moment when you were on stage. . .."

Sarah blushed. "It was nothing. I thought I saw someone in the crowd that I didn't want to see, but I can't be sure it was him."

"Is someone harassing you?" Blue asked.

"Not anymore. I took out a restraining order and so far, I haven't had any more problems."

"Oh, come here." Eryn held out her arms.

"Listen, you need to tell us if someone is bothering you. Okay?" Eryn hugged her.

"I hate to impose and I'm sure it is nothing. I just don't feel like being alone in the crowd tonight."

"And you won't be, stay here with us and enjoy the view and tell me what happened." Blue said.

Eryn smiled at his comforting tone.

"Well, before I worked for Eryn, I worked in a large legal firm and there was a guy who work in IT. He seemed nice enough, a bit of a geek and he didn't seem to have many friends. He asked me to lunch once and I went and then on a couple of dates, but he was a little too odd for me and I refused to go out with him anymore. He wouldn't accept no for an answer and got possessive like, and he kept following me around town and he would say things like I just didn't understand and that we were meant to be together. The final straw was he followed me home one night and was being aggressive verbally, not physically. He never tried to force himself on me, but he was yelling and one of my neighbors called the police, then he really went nuts when the police got there. One of the officers convinced me to take out a restraining order and that seems to have worked. So far anyway."

Blue listened intently. He took out his phone and started taking notes.

"What is this guy's name?"

"Robert Porter."

"Where does he work?"

"The last place I knew him from was the law firm, Joyner and Freeman."

"Okay." Blue nodded.

"I don't want to make trouble for him unnecessarily. He might not have been him in the crowd tonight."

"No need to take chances." Eryn squeezed her hand.

"Has he tried contacting you through email or by phone or anything?" Blue asked.

"No, I installed a security system in my apartment. But I haven't had any further contact."

Blue smiled. "Well, then perhaps he got the message. But, if you see him do not hesitate to call 911 or me, don't take any chances."

"Okay."

"So how did you like your first fashion show?" Eryn changed the subject.

"It is crazy!" They laughed and accepted more drinks from a passing waiter.

Chapter Nine

Blue sat on the deck of his boat bobbing in the water at the downtown marina.

"Permission to come aboard?" Chuck called out.

"Come ahead." Blue called back raising his beer in Chuck's direction.

"Hey man, I brought re-enforcements." Chuck held up a six pack.

"You're a good man." Blue laughed. "Put them in the cooler and grab a cold one."

Chuck did as he was told and sunk down in the chair next to Blue.

"Not seeing Eryn today?"

"No, maybe later. She is working."

Chuck shook his head, "Wow, that girl works more than you do."

Blue chuckled.

"How's it going?" Chuck asked.

"Okay."

"I don't mean in general I mean with you and Eryn." Chuck pegged him with a stare.

"Still, okay."

Chuck studied his friend and took a long pull from the beer. "Look man, I can tell she is special. I can see the way you look at her. So why are you holding back?"

"What makes you think I'm holding back?"

"Does she know you have a boat?"

"No."

"Why not?"

"Hasn't really come up."

"That is a lame ass excuse. It's pretty easy to work into a conversation."

"Really?"

"Yeah, you could say, 'Eryn how about you ditch work on Saturday, and we go out on my boat?'"

"You have it all worked out, huh?"

"No, but I do have more worked than you."

"I am taking it slow."

"Why didn't you invite her the unit party."

"Because I don't go to the family and friend's day. You know that and why are we talking about this again?"

"Because you didn't have a family or friend to take with you, now you do."

"Look Chuck, I got this."

"You do now, I just don't want you to lose it."

"What makes you think I'm going to lose Eryn."

"Because you are going to keep her at arm's length and not let her all the way in."

Blue considered Chuck for a moment. He knew is friend was right, but he hadn't worked out how he was going to handle this relationship. It had been a long time and too many things had happened, that he wasn't sure he was prepared to share or burden someone with his demons.

"Chuck we've been out half a dozen times. It is a little early to gauge how long this will last or how deep it is going to go."

"It can go as deep as you want it to. I can tell you unless you open up and let her in, it isn't going to go very far. But, hey if you're comfortable with losing a woman like that, no problem."

"What do you mean?" Blue looked at him suspiciously.

"I mean if you don't want her. I'll be happy to share my life with her."

Chuck had no intention of dating Eryn, but he knew Blue felt strongly for her even if he wasn't willing to admit to himself.

"The hell you will."

Chuck laughed. "That's what I thought."

"Shut up and drink your beer." Blue turned his attention back to the water and thought about what Chuck had said.

Chuck only let him enjoy the view for a new minutes before he stood up. "Hey, are we going to do some fishing or what?"

"Yeah, okay." Blue got up and went to the controls and fired up the dual inboards and slowly motored out of the marina to a spot near the Chesapeake Bay Bridge tunnel.

"If you manage to catch anything worth keeping, I'll cook it up." Chuck challenged.

"You're going to be busy tonight."

Blue cast his line and waited. He and Chuck had a standing competition as to who could catch the most fish and the largest.

Blue was piloting his boat back into the marina when his phone buzzed with a text from Eryn.

"Just wanted to say, hi."

"How would you like to meet me at the marina for dinner?"

"Is Chuck cooking?"

"As a matter of fact, he is."

"I'm in."

"Okay, I'm at the downtown marina, on pier nine, look for a boat named Dream Catcher."

"A boat?"

"Yeah, do you get seasick? It will be tied up."

"No," Eryn laughed. I don't get seasick. "I just didn't know you had a boat."

"Oh yeah, well I'm full of surprises."

"Yes, you are."

He slid the phone back in his pocket.

"Chuck, good thing I caught extras, Eryn is coming for dinner."

"Maybe I should split, so you can have some privacy."

"No, she knows you're here. In fact, she wanted to make sure you were cooking."

Chuck winked at his friend. "Maybe she likes me better than she likes you after all."

"Shut up."

Chuck laughed as he pulled out more fish to clean.

"I'm going to take a shower." Blue announced.

"A shower?"

"Yeah, I don't want to smell like fish guts when Eryn gets here."

"Whatever man."

Blue went below decks and pulled a change of clothes from his stash on the boat and went to shower.

"Hello!" Eryn called when she found the boat.

"Come aboard!" Chuck answered then stepped over to the rail. "Here let me give you a hand."

"Thank you."

"I'm glad you could join us; pretty boy is down below." Chuck smiled.

"Is this your boat or Blue's?"

"Oh, it's Blue's. Wanna beer?"

"Sure."

Chuck grabbed a bottle from the cooler. "This one, okay?"

"Oh, yeah, that's fine." She looked around.

"Blue will be up in a minute. We've been fishing all afternoon and he wanted to clean up before you got here."

She nodded. "It's a very nice boat."

"Thank you." Blue stepped out on the deck and walked over to Eryn.

"Hi." Eryn smiled.

"Glad you could come." Blue leaned in and kissed her on the cheek. "I see Chuck is being a good temporary host."

She raised her beer. "He is."

Blue nodded to the seats on the stern.

"Want sit down?"

"Sure."

"How was your day?"

"Oh, the usual, retail business is busier on the weekends lots of people with questions about what to plant, how to care for them, that sort of thing."

"You really need to get some help."

"I have help, we were all busy today."

Blue leaned back and put his arm around her shoulders. Eryn leaned into him.

"It is a beautiful sunset." She said dreamily.

"Yes."

Chuck busied himself in the galley prepping vegetables for the grill along with the fish.

"Have you always boated?"

"Well, not as often as I'd like. But I have always enjoyed boats yes."

"I can't believe you didn't mention that before."

Blue shrugged Chucks words echoing in his mind.

"I don't know, I guess I was too busy learning about you."

He watched as a curious look passed across Eryn's face. The kind of look that let him know she didn't quite believe him but was willing to take him at his word.

"All good things come to those who wait." She offered.

Blue frowned at her.

"Just means it takes time to get to know someone." She smiled.

"Yes. It does."

"Okay, love birds, dinner is ready." Chuck stepped up on to the deck and carried plates over to a table.

"Come on." Blue nudged her.

"Chuck this looks amazing, you guys caught this today?"

"I caught the fish; Chuck spent the afternoon losing bait."

Eryn laughed at their banter.

"Keep it up tough guy, wait til she finds out you can't cook at all and she dumps you and your flashy boat for a man who can cook." Chuck laughed but the meaning wasn't lost on Blue.

"I don't need a man to cook for me." Eryn piped up. "I can cook for us both."

Blue smiled at her.

"Besides," Eryn gave Blue a sideways glance, "I already know he can cook breakfast."

Chuck looked at Blue in surprise, "Oh well, then I guess you're all set, buddy." Chuck raised in beer in a toast to Blue.

Eryn sensed there was something more to this topic between the two men, but she decided to stay out of it.

Sarah, was exhausted and turned down Penn's invitation for brunch on Sunday. Things had been a whirlwind lately and she was still a little shaken about seeing Rob in the crowd at the fashion show. It was a public forum and there wasn't anything she could do about that. He was free to be there and he hadn't made any sort of attempt to contact her. He didn't even acknowledge her when she saw him. But she was sure it was him, despite what she had told Eryn and Blue. She stayed home with the door locked. She needed some down time. Work had been busy, and she was more involved with the business than she had ever been with any of their other jobs. It was exciting but draining at the same time. She brewed a cup of breakfast tea and sat down with some toast and a book.

Rob kept his laptop up on the social media page so he could see if Sarah logged in. He really wanted to talk to her and find out why she had been modeling at the fashion show Friday night. Was it something she was getting into now? Parading around in front of people. He had been glad there hadn't been anything too skimpy involved. He still didn't like the idea of sharing her with everyone else. He didn't like the idea of other guys ogling her even if she was fully clothed. Did she do it for the money? When they were married, he would make enough money so she couldn't have to work jobs like that at night after working all day. She would be free to stay home with the children.

After dinner Chuck cleaned up the dishes and said his goodbyes to Eryn.

"Thank you for dinner, it was wonderful." Eryn squeezed his hand.

"Anytime." He smiled and then looked over at Blue. "I'll see ya."

Blue nodded. "See ya."

They watched at Chuck's large athletic frame strode up the pier to the parking lot.

"Everything okay with you two?" Eryn turned to Blue.

"Yeah, why?"

"Felt like maybe there was a little tension tonight."

"Chuck is just mad he lost a bet to me again."

"What kind of bet?"

"Who could catch more fish." Blue laughed.

"Do you normally win?"

"I always win, that is why he is so upset."

Eryn laughed. She didn't doubt that Blue didn't do anything and everything he set his mind to doing.

"You both seem like pretty competitive guys; how often do you butt heads?"

"I wouldn't call it butting heads, exactly."

"Oh?"

"No, Chuck is good at a lot of things, he is even better than me at few of them, just not everything."

"For example."

"You really aren't going to let this go, are you?"

"No, and I'll tell you why."

Blue stepped in front of her to look deep into her eyes. "Okay, tell me."

"Because, I think it has something to do with me. And if I'm wrong, I'll be truly embarrassed, but I want you tell me that I am way off base."

Blue sighed and looked past her. He rested his chin on the top of her head for a moment.

"No, you're not wrong."

"Okay," she nodded. "I don't want to pressure into something you don't want to do. But I don't want to be the cause of a rift between you and your friend."

"There's no rift. He just has a different way of doing things."

"Like relationships?"

"Yes, like relationships."

"So how is his approach different than yours?"

Blue signed again. "Chuck is an all in kinda guy, it's all or nothing with him, damn the torpedoes and all of that."

"And you are a little more cautious."

"Yes."

She nodded.

"He thinks that I am not moving fast enough in our relationship and that I will lose you if I don't move it along."

"Move it along how?" She hoped he didn't mean physically because she wasn't sure she was ready for that yet.

"He thinks I am holding back because I didn't tell you about the boat before today."

She looked puzzled.

"He's upset over the boat?"

"Yeah."

"That is a little weird."

"That's what I said."

"What is his rationale for that argument."

"Something along the lines of me not opening up to you as completely as I should, and the boat is a symptom of that."

"Wow, that's pretty deep."

"Yeah."

He walked the over to the stern seating to watch the moon rise over the water.

"Well, I am a little surprised you didn't mention it when we were talking about my surfing or you playing golf. But I guess I understand why you don't belong to the country club; this is a pretty expensive hobby."

Blue chuckled. "Well, I thought I'd sound like I was bragging."

Eryn laughed out loud. "Well, I think you should brag about your boat, it's pretty nice and I've seen a few boats in my life."

Blue pulled her close.

"So, you're impressed, huh?"

She knew he was joking. "Oh yeah." She widened her eyes in a dramatic fashion.

Blue laughed. "Then that is all that matters."

"You know I care about you and not your boat or car or any of that stuff, right?" Eryn asked suddenly concerned.

"I know that." He hugged her.

They sat watching the moon in silence for a while.

"Eryn?"

"Yes?"

"I care about you more than I have cared for anyone in a very long time."

She leaned back away from him so she could see him more clearly.

"But it scares the hell out of me." He admitted.

Her heart was beating wildly. She wanted to tell him that she really cared about him too, but maybe even loved him. She certainly hadn't felt about anyone like this before and she honestly couldn't imagine what her life would be like without him. He wasn't threatened by her independence and didn't complain when she worked long hours or weekends. But she could sense he was hesitant to commit to anything and she could certainly understand about being gun shy about relationships.

"Blue, this relationship is between you and me and no one else. And we can take it as slow as you and I feel we need to, I don't want you to feel pressured and I don't want us to rush into anything. But I honestly don't remember what life was like before I met you."

Blue stood up and pulled her to her feet. He cupped his hands on her face and slowly kissed her.

Her heart started doing summersaults as she returned the kiss.

"Eryn." Blue whispered against her cheek.

"I'd never do anything to hurt you."

"I know." She whispered. She kissed his cheek.

He kissed her again. Then they sank back to the cushioned seats. "Be patient with me?" He whispered.

"Of course."

He pulled back and looked at her searching and found the sincerity in her yes. He smiled.

The sound of voices coming down the pier broke the spell and Blue sat up.

Eryn felt breathless and she wasn't sure if she was glad for the interruption or disappointed.

"Eryn." Blue held her hands. "Will you stay tonight; we can stay above deck."

She could tell by his eyes that he just didn't want to be alone tonight, and she truly understood how that felt.

"Yes, I will stay."

"I'll be right back," He disappeared below and returned with blankets off the bed. He scooted them back so they could stretch their legs out and then wrapped her in his arms. They laid there lulled by the slapping of the water against the hull and the moon light dancing on the water. She couldn't remember when she had felt more at peace.

She closed her eyes and wondered if this was all real. A man who wasn't in a hurry to jump in bed with her. He didn't mind enjoying moments like this. She was grateful to find out if they were compatible on this level before committing to a physical relationship. Something so intimate meant something to her and she didn't easily share this moment with just anyone. She didn't know how long this would last but she was going to enjoy it while it did. But the was also afraid. Afraid that enjoying it would lead her to a path that break her heart again. She knew she was strong enough to recover, but she wasn't sure she wanted to put herself in that situation. But Blue might actually be worth it.

He stirred beneath her, and then settled she could tell by his breathing he was asleep. She smiled to herself and whispered.

"You sleep I'll keep watch."

She wondered how often he slept well. His job was beyond stressful. His past seemed to be filled with mysterious and painful memories. She would watch over him tonight hopefully the way he had watched over his friends like Chuck in the past. Eryn dozed on and off, but she was awake when the first streaks of daylight painted the morning sky. Blue was still asleep, and she wondered if she should go below and try to find a way to make coffee. She shivered slightly in the predawn air and Blue stirred.

"Hey" His voice was rough with sleep.

She turned her face to look at him. "Hey."

"Have we been out here all night?"

"Yeah." She smiled.

"Oh, you must be freezing."

"No actually I'm fine."

He started to sit up. He tilted his head left and right to stretch his neck muscles. He smiled at her and kissed her lightly. "Are you okay?" He asked.

"Couldn't be better."

"Want some coffee?"

"Yes."

"Come below and get warm and I'll make us a cup."

He stood and she followed him into the galley.

It was nicer than her kitchen at home.

"This is a very impressive boat."

"And I'm sure you're wondering how I can afford it.?

"That is none of my business."

"Its okay, I get asked that a lot especially by internal affairs types."

"Are you serious?"

"It comes up occasionally.

"Anyway, it was owned by a pretty nasty guy who we arrested, and we seized his assets. After a time, some of those assets went up for auction I bought the boat then."

"Does it bother you that a bad guy owned it?"

"Not really. I had it inspected and had it thoroughly cleaned. But I think of it as a win for the good guys." He laughed. "Does it bother you?"

Eryn thought about it for a moment. She didn't know the specifics of what the boat was used for, she thought it was better she didn't know. She wondered how she would feel if she knew someone was killed on it or something. But, decided she agreed with Blue. A bad guy was caught and now his boat belonged to a good man and that was okay.

"No, I'm not bothered by it."

Blue smiled. "Okay."

He poured her a cup of coffee and that sat inside and watched the sunrise.

"Eryn, if there is ever anything about my job that you have questions about or that bothers you, I want you to let me know okay?"

She looked at him and wondered if that is what had happened to his past relationships, someone wasn't able to handle his day job.

"Okay." She nodded.

"I mean it, if I can't tell you something it is because its something of a security nature, but I will always be honest with you."

"Fair enough."

He nodded and looked out the expansive window.

"The same goes for you." She added.

"Hmm?"

"You know if you ever have concerns about my job. You know some of those plants are poisonous."

He wondered if she was serious for a moment and then started laughing.

Eryn laughed with him.

"Agreed." He raised his coffee cup in a toast.

The sun was promising a beautiful day.

"You can't beat this view." Blue observed.

"No, you can't." She turned to see he was staring at her.

She smiled then noticed the hands on his wristwatch. She grabbed his arm and pulled it to her.

"Is it six o'clock?"

He glanced at his wrist.

"Zero six hundred."

"I have to go!" She jumped up.

"Eryn! Sit down and finish your coffee." He insisted.

She blinked in his direction.

"I have to go home and shower and change."

"The shop will be there when you get there. I'm sure your employees are capable of starting their day on their own."

"Yes, they are but. . ."

"But nothing you are always rushing off. Sit, enjoy the sunrise, you're going to miss something important running around like this all the time."

She stared at him and slowly lowered herself back into the chair. He had a point. But she wasn't fully comfortable with this attitude either.

"What about you?" She asked.

"My office knows how to find me if they need me before I get there."

She wasn't as reassured as she thought she would be with his answer. She frowned.

He laughed.

"Go, but we are going to work on this. Trust me. I know what I am talking about."

She stood up to take her cup to the sink.

"Leave it. I'll get it."

"No, I . . ."

He stepped around the table and placed his hand over hers and took the cup and set it on the table.

"There are more important things than the cup."

His voice was a whisper. She was mesmerized by his eyes again. She didn't have enough breath to answer him.

He bent down and kissed her passionately. Her body was responding in ways she wished it wouldn't, not when she had to go to work. If he had kissed her like that last night who knows what might have happened.

When he pulled back. She was weak in the knees.

"Now go to work, Eryn but promise me you will think about what is important in life."

With that he stepped back and released her.

"I will." She squeaked.

She headed for the dock, still breathless.

She looked back as she stepped onto the pier.

He was standing there watching her, the look in his eyes left her no question as to what would have happened if she had chosen to stay after that kiss.

Blue returned her wave.

As she drove home, she wondered what would be the worst that could happen if she was late for work, or took a day off?

Blue had her all mixed up. Would he have stayed with her on the boat this morning? Yes, of course he would have she could tell by the look his eyes.

She had been so focused and driven on the business for so long she didn't how to handle this new situation. But clearly, she needed to figure it out because if this relationship was going to work with Blue, it was going to involve letting go and focusing on things other than mulch orders, broken pumps and payroll. But she couldn't let a business she had worked so hard to build just fall apart. What if things didn't work out with Blue and then she'd have to clean up whatever shambles her business had turned into while she was focused on a man.

No, she couldn't let that happen. But what was wrong with enjoying life? She used to enjoy life, she used to be so carefree, traveling, surfing she didn't own anything, and nothing owned her. Now, she was so busy with the business she didn't have any friends beyond Penn and now Sarah. She hadn't allotted a space for a romantic relationship and now she wasn't sure how she was going to fit one into her plans.

Blue hadn't given her an ultimatum, but it was clear he wanted more.

She arrived home without even remembering the drive. She went through the motions of showering, grabbing a cereal bar and driving to work. She was only a few minutes late, but the greenhouse staff that had already arrived were already busy at work, others were still coming in. Sarah was there and everything seemed to be running smoothly. She was fifteen minutes late and the world had not fallen apart.

She walked around the green houses and then outside to start watering and checking on the outdoor plants.

Several hours later, Eryn made her way back to her office. Her stomach rumbled.

"Hey, how's it going?" Sarah greeted as she met her at the door.

"Good." Eryn smiled. "You headed out?"

"Just stepping out to grab lunch for myself and the retail shop crew, you want anything?"

"Yes, actually."

Eryn fished cash out of jeans pocket.

"Where are you headed?"

"Sub shop, is that okay?"

"Yeah, can you bring me back a turkey and cheese sub?"

"No problem, anything else?"

"No that should be fine."

"Okay, be back shortly."

Eryn went to her office and sank into her old beaten desk chair. It had seen better days. But it was comfortable even though she was sure it was going to collapse at any moment.

She pulled out her phone and laid it on the desk. No text or calls from Blue today. She refused to admit that she was curious as to why. He wasn't the clingy type, but she thought she might have heard from him by now.

She logged into her computer and looked at her email, then the local newspaper. Then she knew why she hadn't heard from Blue. He was giving a brief press conference about a disabled man who had been killed and drug from his wheelchair and stuffed in an old, abandoned freezer. There had been other shootings overnight and a police officer injured. He was busy today and she couldn't expect him to stop what he was doing to text her.

Instead, she sent him a text.

"Thinking of you today. Saw the news. I'm here for you."

She put the phone back down. She didn't expect or need a reply.

She closed her eyes for just a moment. She hadn't slept much lately. She didn't feel as tired as she thought she should.

"Eryn?"

She jumped startled. "What?"

"Hey, it's just me. I have your lunch." Sarah was standing at the door way holding a bag.

"Oh. Thank you." Eryn sat up straight. "Sorry I must have dozed off."

"Are you okay?"

"Yeah, just don't seem to be getting much sleep lately."

"You want to talk about it."

"Oh, it's not anything to worry about. I just need to manage my time better." Eryn tried to laugh it off. "Sit down if you like." She pointed to the guest chair.

Sarah handed her a plain white paper bag and then sat down and opened her own bag.

"Let me get us some soda from the fridge."

"I'll get them, I'm closer."

Sarah got up and returned with two cold cans of soda.

"I got some fries too." Sarah pulled them from her bag and sat them between on the desk.

Eryn opened her bag and retrieved her sandwich. Her stomach rumbled she was starving.

She took a bite and savored it. After one more bite from her sandwich and a couple of fries she felt human again.

"So how is everything with you?" She asked Sarah.

"Good."

"What about that guy you thought you saw at the fashion show? Any problems?"

"No, I haven't heard from him or seen him anywhere. But I hate feeling so paranoid. It makes me so angry."

Eryn had never had a stalker or a problematic boyfriend in that way. She couldn't imagine, what it must be like, but she could empathize.

"I just don't understand who someone can do that to another human being."

"I'm afraid I don't have an answer for that, other than to say the world is getting to be a very scary place these days. I don't know if it is that I am more aware of what is going on in the world or what."

"What do you mean?"

"When Penn and I were young, we traveled the world with hardly any money. We worked when we needed to at whatever jobs we could get. We slept in tents on the beach or on someone's couch and we never worried about anyone causing us any harm. Not everyone welcomed us, some thought we were tramps or hippies or something. But they never tried to do us harm and we just moved on until we found people more like ourselves."

Sarah sat staring wide-eyed her sandwich forgotten. Listening with awe as Eryn spoke.

"Are you serious?"

Eryn laughed. "Yes, I'm serious."

"Okay, wait a minute," Sarah held up her hands and closed her eyes for a moment. "You mean to tell me, that Penn, used to tend bar and live in a tent?"

Eryn's laugh was louder this time. "Girl, I can tell you some stories about Penn."

"Wow, I just am having a hard time imagining that."

"Yes, well like I said before she was different before she went to Milan."

"I guess so, I mean I didn't doubt you I guess I just didn't realize the change was that extreme."

"She'd do it again in a heartbeat trust me."

"Wow, that sounds like a lot of fun. I wish I could do something like that."

"It was a different time back then. We didn't have to worry about being stalked or kidnapped, murdered or any of those things you hear about happening to young woman on vacation these days."

"That is true." Eryn sighed her thoughts going back to Rob.

"So how are things going with Blue?"

Eryn blushed. "Fine."

"Whoa! Really?"

"What?"

"Your face is red as a beet." Sarah laughed and then leaned closer and whispered. "Did you sleep with him?"

"No!"

"But you want to." Sarah leaned back in her chair and munched a French fry.

"No, well yes, but not tonight." Eryn stammered.

"Why not?"

"Well, because I don't know. Too soon?"

"Too soon from a carefree spirit that has surfed the world living in tents on the beach. Really?" Sarah gave her a doubtful look.

"I want it to mean something."

"Okay." Sarah pretended to concentrate on her food.

Eryn sat back and sipped her soda. Was she being too much of a prude? She had never slept around, but she wasn't a virgin either. Maybe she needed to rethink her attitude towards Blue.

He had implied he felt the same way she did but, she was sure he also felt physically attracted to her. The kissing had proven that.

Chapter Ten

B lue missed talking to Eryn, but there was just too much going on at work and there was no time. He thought about calling her late, but he had kept her out late hours several nights and he really wanted her to get some sleep. God knows he needed it. Before he went home, he drove to the Seabreeze and walked into the bar. It was late and there was probably only an hour before last call. He was grateful the place was empty.

"What will you have?"

"Bud."

The bartender nodded. And pulled a mug from the shelf and pulled the beer from the tap.

Blue nodded his thanks and put a five-dollar bill down on the bar. He waived off the change and the bartender sensing he wanted to be alone moved to the other end of the bar to busy himself.

"Drinking alone is a very bad sign."

Chuck's voice broke into Blue's train of thought.

"Not necessarily."

"In your case it usually is."

Chuck sat down next to him. The bartender brought him a club soda without asking.

"Just a long day. I thought his might help me sleep."

"Yeah, I saw the news."

"It doesn't get any easier. You'd think it would, but it doesn't."

"Why do you keep doing it?" Chuck looked at his friend. "I'd thought you'd seen enough killing and evil already."

Blue just shook his head and finished his beer.

"You talk to Eryn today?"

Blue shook his head. "No, just a couple of text messages."

Chuck nodded. He understood. It was the same when they had fought in the Middle East. They both had been married when they went over and they didn't tell their wives about what they saw, they didn't want to bring the ugliness home. Home was their place of refuge and to talk about the things they saw would ruin that. The war had lasted longer than both their marriages. Blue had showed little interest in serious relationships after that, throwing himself into his work. But Eryn seemed to be changing that and Chuck was cautiously optimistic.

Blue drank a second beer in silence. When he was done Chuck came back into the bar.

"I'll give you a ride home."

"Okay."

A waitress walked out with them.

Blue raised his eyebrows at Chuck.

"She'll drive my car and follow us to your house. Then I'll take her home."

"Sure." Blue shook his head. Chuck enjoyed the company of women, but never seemed interested in serious relationships. He rarely dated anyone more than a few months. Which seemed to be mutual he enjoyed having a good time and when both parties were bored, they both moved on, no hard feelings.

Eryn went home exhausted. She had been operating on less sleep than normal and she was wiped out. Blue had too much on his plate, she didn't press him for conversation today. She was too tired, and he was too busy.

She went home and made a grilled cheese sandwich and flopped down on the sofa. She watched TV for nearly an hour before heading to bed. She checked her phone one last time and set her alarm. It was ten o'clock and she fell asleep immediately.

Six in the morning came too quickly. But she did at least feel somewhat refreshed. She made coffee and took it back upstairs while she showered and dressed.

She was the first to arrive at the nursery. She parked and closed the car door with her hip while carrying her coffee and keys to the door. A movement out the corner of her eye caught her attention. She stopped and looked around. She didn't see anyone, but she had a shiver move down her spine. She wondered if she was interrupting someone about to break into the shop. She tried to act natural, but she hurried to the door and it seemed to take forever for the key to work in the lock. Once inside she relocked the door and kept the lights off. She stepped back into the shadows of the store and watched the parking lot. There was someone near the street, but she couldn't be sure that is who she had seen or heard. She watched as they crossed the street to the drug store.

She breathed a sigh of relief and relaxed a bit. She turned to go to her office and screamed.

A man was standing right behind her. He was so close she couldn't figure how he had gotten in without her knowing. The door had been locked. Had she reset the alarm? She couldn't remember. It should have gone off regardless.

"Shhh" He put a gloved hand over her mouth.

She dropped her coffee and started kicking. Despite his thin stature the man was surprisingly strong. Her vision got cloudy, and she was certain she smelled something odd on his glove. She knew she should be able to name the smell, but her brain was fuzzy, and she couldn't think right now. She felt like she was moving but she didn't feel her legs working.

She watched as items passed by her vision as she was drug to the back of the store to the employee entrance. She tried to kick and scream some more. But her body felt sluggish, and the room was getting dark.

Sarah saw Eryn's car in the parking lot and shook her head, it didn't matter how early she got to work, Eryn was always here first.

The door was locked, which wasn't unusual if Eryn had been here alone for any length of time. She was safety conscious. Sarah unlocked the door and went inside. The alarm was off, and no lights were on. Maybe Eryn was in the green houses or something.

"Eryn! You here?"

She checked Eryn's office and then walked upfront and slipped in something wet.

Sarah gasped as she saw Eryn's keys and coffee cup spilled on the floor. She raced back to her office, her heart pounding and called the police.

She answered the 911 operators' questions.

"Ma'am are you sure no one else is there?"

"No, I'm not sure. I haven't been out to the green houses yet."

"Could your boss be there?"

"And leave a spilled coffee cup and her keys laying in the middle of the floor?" Sarah was starting to get hysterical.

"We are sending someone to your location. I need you to stay..."

Sarah clicked off, she didn't have time for the 911 operators instructions. She needed to call Blue and then Penn. Or maybe Penn then Blue. She was in full panic mode. She dialed Blue's number from the business card he gave her as she headed for the green houses. Calling out Eryn's name.

"Hello."

"Blue?"

"Yes, who's this?"

"This is Sarah, I work with Eryn, you said I could call you..."

"What's wrong Sarah?" Blue could hear she was panicked. "Is someone trying to hurt you?"

"No, Eryn!"

"What?"

"I think something has happened to Eryn." She said and then looked around the greenhouse and called out Eryn's name.

"Sarah, Sarah! Listen to me." Blue tried to get her to focus. While he grabbed his service weapon and the car keys. "What happened?"

"I came to work. Eryn's car is here but she isn't. I found spilled office and her keys on the floor."

"Listen to me, I want you to go to a safe place, a closet or an office and lock yourself inside."

"I have to find Eryn."

"Do you hear me, get yourself to a safe place. I am on my way."

He was already putting the car in drive.

"Okay." Sarah clicked off and ran back to the offices.

Blue's car was unmarked, but he had lights in the grill and a siren. He turned them all on as he raced towards the nursery. He called dispatch from the car's police radio.

"We have a unit arriving on scene now, Chief."

"10-4, show me at the scene."

"10-4."

Blue pulled in behind the marked car.

The uniformed officers were knocking on the glass door. Blue called Sarah back on her cell.

"Sarah, it's Blue I'm outside can you come open the door?"

"Okay."

She stepped carefully around the keys and spilled coffee to open the front door for the police.

The two officers and Blue stepped inside.

"Sarah, tell us what happened." Blue took the lead.

"I saw Eryn's car in the parking lot which is not unusual. I went around to the side employee entrance."

The uniformed officers were making notes.

"When I didn't see her in the back, I called out for her and I came up here and saw that." She pointed to the floor.

The two officers walked over to inspect the floor.

"And you are sure these are the owner's keys?" One of the officers asked.

"Yes."

Fresh tears dampened Sarah's face.

"Okay, then what?" Blue tried to get her to refocus.

"I called 911, then I went to the green houses while I was calling you."

Her voice wavered but she was holding it together for the moment.

"Then I went and locked myself in my office, like you said."

Blue nodded and put his hands on her shoulders.

"You did good." He steered her towards the back.

"Why don't you sit down and take a deep breath while the officers and I have a look around, okay?"

She nodded and sniffled.

The other employees started to arrive and Blue, and the officers began questioning everyone. When they were done, they were not better off than when they started.

"No one knew of anyone that would want to harm Eryn. No irate customers, no ex-boyfriends, even the two employees who had been questioned after the break-in hadn't held a grudge. They effectively had nothing to go on.

Blue heard a car pull into the parking lot and the sound of tires squealing. A moment later Penn burst into the shop.

"What is going on? Where is Eryn, where is Sarah?"

"Penn, calm down"

Penn was more hysterical than Sarah had been earlier. "I got a call from Sarah that Eryn is missing?"

"Penn!" Sarah came running across the shop.

"Sarah, what is going on?"

"I found Eryn's keys and spilled coffee when I came in this morning but no Eryn."

Penn looked at Blue.

"What are you doing here? Why are you out looking for her?"

"Penn, I am trying to determine who would harm her."

"No one would harm her; how can you even ask that question? You've been dating her you know what a sweet person she is, why would someone want to harm her."

Blue waited while she vented.

"A person who isn't rational like you and I, someone who sees the world differently than the rest of us."

"I'm sorry, I know you're doing your best."

Blue didn't feel like that was a compliment and he watched quietly as Penn and Sarah went back to Sarah's office.

"Sir,"

"Yes, officer."

"We've finished taking all the statement from the employees working today."

"Thank you, we'll let the detectives take it from here."

"Yes, sir."

The officer left him alone with his thoughts. The situation didn't feel random to him. If the alarm system was off and there was no evidence of forced entry, then maybe the person came in behind Eryn? And which door had she come in? He thought the front door because of where the keys and coffee were found.

"Sarah!" He called out as he walked to her office.

"Yes?"

"You said you came in the employee entrance, right?"

"Yes."

"Was it locked?"

"Yes." Her voice was weak.

"Are you sure?"

She sat thinking about it for several minutes. Trying to relive the moment in her head.

"No, it wasn't but the alarm was on."

"What are you getting at?" Penn asked.

"Why would Eryn put the alarm but and leave the door unlocked. Wouldn't it be the opposite?"

"You're right!" Sarah jumped up.

"So, you think someone tried to cover up their tracks but turning on the alarm, but they didn't have Eryn's keys to lock the door?" Penn asked.

"I'm not sure, what I think at the moment."

"Who has access to the alarm system?"

"Me, Eryn and Ryan who is the green house manager and comes in early. And of course, the alarm company."

"Do you all use the same code, or do you have personalized codes?"

"The same as far as I know." Sarah slumped back down.

"Okay, thanks."

"Wait, that's it?" Penn was on her feet.

"No, that is not it, but it is all I can do from here."

He let his irritation show and he shouldn't have but he was on a mission, and he couldn't get it done standing around here.

On his way out Blue ran into Detective Graham Fisher.

"Chief."

"Detective."

"I understand you have some sort of personal interest in this case?" Fisher sounded like he was questioning Blue.

"I do, the missing woman is my girlfriend and I want her found."

"Okay, sir, but I need to ask you a few questions."

"Not right now."

"But sir. You know the drill I have to question anyone who has had contact with the victim."

Blue turned on him and cut him off.

"Why don't you look into people who might use her as a way to get to me?"

"That is certainly one angle worth exploring, but I have to look at every possible...."

"Detective. I know how this works. So why don't you stop by my office later and I will answer your questions, right now I have a lead I need to follow up on."

"But sir...."

"My office this afternoon."

Blue walked away. He didn't much care how it looked that he refused to answer questions at the moment. He had bigger things on his mind, and he would deal with the detective later.

"Sir, at least let me get you a detail." Fisher called after him.

Blue waived him off and sped out of the parking lot. Blue used his car's navigation to find the local office for the security company.

"Yes, sir can I help you?" The security guard in the lobby greeted him.

Blue produced his badge and ID.

"I'm Chief of police and I need to talk to someone who help me determine if an alarm system was been tampered with it is part of a possible kidnapping case."

"Yes. Sir!" The guard picked up the phone and punched in a number.

"Someone will right down to help you."

"Thank you."

Blue waited impatiently for the elevator to chime announcing the arrival of someone.

"Chief?"

"Yes."

"I'm Amanda Ross, I can help you if you come with me."

"Thank you."

"You say this is a possible kidnapping?"

"Yes, from a commercial location. I was hoping we could see who accessed the system and at what time."

"A lot depends on the type of system at the location but hopefully we can find some way to help."

"I'd really appreciate that."

He followed her into a large room full of cubicles.

"Excuse me, Jeffrey can you come with me for a moment I need your assistance."

"Yes, ma'am."

The young man looked like he was all of twelve years old. He was reed thin and gangly. He was pale from a lack of sunlight which Blue found common in the younger generation.

They walked into an empty office with a desk and a computer.

"What is the name of the business?"

"Sandcastle Nursery."

"Jeffery, we need to pull up the activity for the alarm system for that business and review it for the last. . .?

"Say eight hours."

"Okay."

The young man's hands flew over the keyboard. Blue couldn't keep up with the movements.

"Looks like the system was deactivated at five forty-five this morning and then reactivated at one minute after six this morning."

"Can you tell by whom?"

"This account doesn't have individual codes so it could be anyone who has the code. Hang on."

Jeffery began typing again, his face inched closer to the monitor. He was mumbling to himself.

Blue looked at Ms. Ross questioningly.

She held up her hand to indicate they would give Jefferey a minute.

"Okay, that's weird." Jeffery said leaning back in the chair.

Blue looked at the monitor nothing on the screen made sense to him.

"What is it?"

"The system was activated remotely both times."

"Is that unusual?"

"It is for this system. It isn't that sophisticated. It didn't come with that option to activate remotely, like setting it from your phone if you forgot to do it before you left or something. This system is an older model and is designed to have the code punched into a keypad."

Blue stared at Jeffrey, "What are you saying?"

"Someone hacked the system."

Blue's blood turned to ice.

"Is there any way to track who might have done that?"

"Yes, but it will take some time and a warrant."

"Okay, listen, I appreciate your help." Blue looked from Jeffery to Ms. Ross.

"Would you mind if I sent a forensic team over here to work what your staff," he indicated Jeffrey. "To help us find this hacker?"

"Not all." Amanda Ross agreed.

"Cool, are you like with the FBI?" Jeffery blinked.

"No, Gates Point police department."

"Wait 'til my mom hears this."

"Let's hold off telling anyone about this until we know who the hacker is and that it is related to our kidnapping case, okay?"

Jeffery nodded pleased to be included in a secret case.

"Mum's the word."

"Thank you."

Blue waited until he was back outside, and he called Detective Fisher to tell him what he had learned at the security company and to ask him to send over his forensic computer team.

"You can stop by my office anytime Detective."

"Be there in ten."

Blue spent the better part of an hour talking with Detective Fisher. And when it was over, he didn't feel like they were any closer to finding out what had happened to Eryn.

The computer team had tried locating by her cell phone but that had been a dead end.

Blue stayed until midnight trying everything, he could think of to find Eryn. He finally gave up and headed for home.

He dialed Chuck's number.

"Hey man, you are stopping by the bar tonight?"

"No, not tonight."

"What's wrong?"

"Eryn is missing."

"What? How?"

"I don't know. I think someone took her."

"What the hell are you talking about? Where are you?"

"Headed home."

"I'll meet you there."

The phone went silent.

Blue and Chuck had been through a lot together. They always had each other's back and if anyone could help him get through this, it was Chuck.

Blue knew Chuck must have broken every traffic law to get to his house at the same time he pulled in his driveway. But he wasn't going to question it tonight.

"What the hell is going on, man?" Chuck asked striding across the front lawn. He was in full kick ass mode.

"I don't know, she was reported missing at 06:30."

Chuck followed Blue inside and went straight for the fridge to get his friend a beer.

"Here, sit down tell me everything."

Chuck set a beer on the coffee table while Blue took off his suit coat and tie and toss them over the back of the sofa.

"Sarah, the bookkeeper found Eryn's keys laying in the floor with a spilled travel mug of coffee, like she was surprised by someone."

"You think someone grabbed her."

"I don't see another explanation." Blue picked up the beer and downed half of it.

Chuck waited.

I went to the security company, and they said that someone hacked into the alarm system and turned it off and then turned its back on.

"So, someone who knew what they were doing."

"Yeah." Blue leaned back and stared at the ceiling.

"Come on Sarge, tell me what you're thinking." Chuck used Blue's military rank.

"Well at first I thought it might be a way for someone to try to get to me, some old enemy or something."

"Sounds reasonable. We made a few back in the day."

"Yeah, but that doesn't feel right."

"What's it feel like?"

"Like something else, something bigger maybe, something more sinister."

"What could be more sinister than some of those people we dealt with in Afghanistan and Libya?"

"No, no, this is closer to home. It's like it is just out of reach like I should know what this is." Blue finished his beer.

"So, what do you want to do?"

"What can I do? I've got exactly jack-nothing-shit to go on." Blue stood up angry.

Chuck sensed there was more than Blue was saying.

"You want another one?" Blue asked heading for the kitchen.

"No, I'm good." Chuck had barely touched his beer. He heard the refrigerator door slam.

"You know what the worst part of this is?"

"What?"

"You were freaking right."

"I'm always right, why is that a bad thing?" Chuck tried to make a joke. But it fell flat.

Blue scowled at him.

"Okay, right about what?"

"I've been holding back with Eryn. I haven't allowed myself to accept the feelings I have for her and I sure as hell haven't told her how I feel. I mean yeah, sure I said that I cared about her, but what does that mean?" Blue ran his hand through his hair.

Chuck had a feeling it was going to come to this, but he remained silent.

"She spent the night on the boat the other night after you left. We sat there looking at the moon and then the sunrise. It was the most perfect night. And I had every opportunity to tell her exactly how I feel about her and what did I do? I fell asleep. I am a complete idiot!"

"Wow, dude, really?"

Blue gave him a glare that would have burned holes in his skull.

"Look all I am saying is that the solution is simple?"

"Oh really, how simple?"

"Save the girl so you can tell her how you feel and stop being a punk."

"Shut up!" Blue didn't laugh, but Chuck could tell the tension was broken.

He leaned back and crossed his legs.

"So, tell me what makes Eryn so damn special?"

Blue looked at him like he had three heads.

"What do you mean?"

"Why is this one worth all this angst."

"You've met her." Blue said as if that would explain everything.

"Sure, I've met her, but I haven't spent as much time with her as you have; so tell me why this one has you tied up in knots."

"She isn't anything like what you expect. Did you know she has won surfing competitions? She's lived on beaches in tents and has a spirit of adventure that you just wouldn't expect from a nursery owner, or at least based on the ones I have met before."

Chuck smiled as Blue talked.

"Well, my man, sounds like this is the one."

"I know and I love that, but why does it terrify me at the same time."

"Because you don't want to screw it up. But I wouldn't worry about it. If she has stuck around this long with you, she probably feels the same way."

"Yeah, maybe." Blue finished off another beer.

"Look why don't you call it a night you aren't going to be any help to Eryn if you keep drinking like that."

"Shit. You're right." Blue stood up and walked to the kitchen to toss the bottle away.

"I'll see ya." Blue said heading for the stairs.

"See ya, man."

Chuck didn't move from his chair. He reached for his beer and took a swig. He'd hang around to make sure his friend was okay.

Eryn opened her eyes. At first it felt like they wouldn't open like they couldn't open. So, she squeezed them tight and then tried again. One then the other cracked open. It was dark wherever she was. She moved her head and could see a sliver of light from under a door. She listened and didn't get the sense that anything thing or anyone was in the room with her.

She slowly sat up and took stock of her body. She felt groggy but nothing felt broken. Her muscles were stiff and a little sore. She wondered how long she had been out. She remembered a hand over her mouth and the smell of something she couldn't place even now. She tried to remember what day it was.

She felt around for any other furnishings and felt a table next to the bed. She felt along the wall and there was a window with a cover stapled over it. She could feel the staples in the windowsill. Then moved further around the room and felt nothing else until she got the door and felt the handle. Her heart pounded as she put her hand on it and thought about turning it. She tried it ever so gently so as not to make any sound. But it wouldn't turn. It was clearly locked. She continued past the door and felt another doorway. And ran her hand along the inside. She found a light switch and turned it on. A bathroom. That was good news. She stepped inside and looked around. There were no toiletries, except for bath tissue. She supposed a razor would have been too much to hope for. She heard footsteps and ran back to the bed and sat down leaving the bathroom light on.

There was a gentle knock at the door and then the handle jiggled as if someone was working the lock before the door opened slowly.

A man stepped inside the room. He looked at her and then the bathroom. He didn't look menacing. In fact, he looked like he be afraid of his own shadow. "Are you okay?"

"Yes. I think so." She replied in a confident voice, trying to hide that fact that she was scared.

"I didn't think you would sleep so long I was starting to get worried."

"Were you the one that grabbed me at the nursery."

"Yes."

"Why?"

"It's all part of my plan and you are going to help me."

"Help you do what? I don't even know you?"

"No, you don't. But I'm a friend of Sarah's and ever since she started working for you, she has been going out drinking and staying out late and doing god knows what else."

She could see he was starting to get agitated. This must be the guy that Sarah said was stalking her.

"So, you are going to help me make it right."

"Okay, well I'm sorry if I caused you any trouble."

He pushed his glasses back up his nose and nodded. He looked like he wanted to believe her but wasn't sure if he should.

"What's your name?"

"Rob."

"Nice to meet you, Rob." She held out her hand.

He studied her for a minute and then shook her hand.

"So, what am I doing here?"

"You are going to help me get Sarah back."

"And how am I going to do that?"

"Well, like I said it is partly your fault that she is ignoring me, and I need her to understand how important it is for us to be together."

"Okay, are you sure about that?"

"Of course, I am sure. I have prayed about it at church."

"And did that help?"

"It helped me to know I am on the right path."

"Why do you think I am to blame?"

"Because it was after she came to work for you that she started staying out late and doing things she wouldn't normally do."

He grabbed his head with both hands. "I've already told you this!"

Eryn backed away trying to stay out of arms reach of him. "How do you know where Sarah goes, do you follow her?"

"Yes, no." He paced back and forth. "I have to keep an eye on her to make sure she is safe and not doing anything crazy just until she realizes we are meant to be together."

"I see."

"No, you don't!"

His moods were swinging wildly from gentle and calm to very aggravated. She wondered if he was on some sort of medication or needed to be.

"Maybe you were meant to be with someone else."

"No! Sarah is the only person who has ever been nice to me and now she is ignoring me and I know it is not her fault it is people like you and the police that are keeping her from me."

"I'm sorry Rob it is not me, I just met you, how could I be keeping her from you if I didn't know you?"

"Shut-up! You're just trying to confuse me!"

He backed out of the bedroom and locked the door.

She took a deep breath. This guy was clearly delusional and unstable. She had to find a way out of her before things escalated.

***

"Thank you for staying with me last night, Penn."

"You're welcome, I think we both needed to not be alone last night."

Sarah and Penn sat at Sarah's second hand dinette table drinking coffee.

"I am going to work today. Eryn wouldn't want the business to be closed."

"No, she wouldn't, and I guess there isn't much we can do anyway."

"I wonder how Blue is doing?"

Penn shook her head. "If there anyone who can do anything about this situation it's Blue."

Sarah nodded in silent agreement.

Each woman left to start their day worried about Eryn.

Chapter Twelve

E ryn stood with her ear pressed against the door, listening. It sounded like her captor was on the computer the sound was muffled but she could make out the sound of keys on a keyboard, as if someone was typing in short bursts. Once in a while she could hear his voice as if he was talking to himself. She laid down on the floor and put her ear against the door hoping to hear something through the small space between the bottom of the door and the floor. It didn't improve things much. Finally, in frustration she stood up and looked around the room. She needed to find a way out of here. She went back to the window and tried to pull back the plastic carefully so it wouldn't be obvious that she was trying to find a way out.

Eryn went to the bathroom and investigated more closely. She needed to find something that would help her send a signal if she couldn't get out of this room. She thought about starting a fire and hoping that someone would see the smoke. But she had no idea where she was and if there was anyone around that would even see it. She didn't need to make things worse for herself and be locked in a closest or basement.

Blue paced his office. He hoped that Ted would come up with something. If there was enough evidence from the transcripts Ted was able to download, then maybe they could get a warrant to track the IP address of the messages. He tried to stay focused on the case and not on Eryn. If he let his thoughts run away with him, he'd run the risk of screwing up the investigation. But he had to admit that this situation had opened his eyes regarding Eryn.

He already knew he enjoyed her company. He had no plans to rush the relationship, but he already knew his life was better with her in it. He wasn't going to let anything mess that up. But he had to let his detectives do their jobs. He couldn't go off halfcocked and try and do this all on his own. He was too close to it, but he was the police chief, and he was damn well going to stay on top of things.

The phone on his desk rang.

"Chief Keegan."

Ted's voice came out in a rush. "Chief, I think I have something."

"I'm on my way."

Blue slammed the phone down and walked to the detective bureau on his way to Ted's office.

"We might have something in the missing person's case." He announced.

"Ted, what do you have?" Blue asked charging through the door.

"I was finally able to trace the IP address. This guy is good, he had it bouncing all over the place, but I think I pinpointed the location." Ted pushed his glasses up on his nose as he talked.

"Are you sure? I need enough evidence for a warrant." Blue continued ignoring the detective in the room.

"I back traced it twice just to make sure."

Blue laid a heavy hand on Ted's shoulder. "Good job." He turned to the detective.

The detective announced as he turned to leave with his cell phone next to his ear. "I'm on it Chief."

"What's the address?" Blue looked down at Ted.

"601 Miriam Court, sir."

Blue smiled down at head, nodded, and left.

Blue met Detective Fisher "So what do we know?" He asked.

"The house is at the end of a cul-de-sac, so tactically an ideal position. There is only one way in or out by car, so we can block that off, but there is a park behind the house, so we need to have that area covered in case he runs out the back."

Blue nodded. "What about defensively? Anything we need to be aware of before we make a frontal assault?"

"I have a plain clothes unit going out to question the neighbors to see if they know anything and to try and provide some reconnaissance."

"Okay, good idea. It will help to know what we might be dealing with before we go in."

"According to the system, this guy has never had so much as a parking ticket."

"Doesn't mean anything, he could be a powder keg of anger and frustration ready to explode."

"Very true." The detective nodded.

They waited for what seemed like an eternity. It took all of Blue's will power to sit there calmly and not charge out the door and go kick some ass. But that would in all likelihood not work as well as he planned, and it might even endanger Eryn. No, he had to let his team do their job.

The detective came back.

"There isn't much to know about our boy. The neighbors say he is quiet and keeps to himself. They haven't seen anyone else around but the say he does keep odd hours, coming and going late at night."

"Could you see anything in the house, lights on in certain rooms?" Blue asked.

"No, all the windows were dark but that would be black out curtains or something on the inside that prevented us from seeing anything."

"So, what's your plan?" Blue asked.

"Well, we are getting our search warrant so I thought we'd try knocking on the door, and if he doesn't let us in, we will let ourselves in."

Blue nodded but didn't say anything he was thinking what the best tactic would be to get Eryn out safely. Unfortunately, they weren't one hundred percent sure she was there, and if she was in the house which room?

Finally, he looked up at the detective.

"Okay, let's go with that. I won't interfere but I'm going with you."

The Detective nodded.

The police rolled into the cul-de-sac very quietly, no lights and no sirens. They staged a couple of units at the end to block an escape down the street and three more units were in the park behind the house with two officers each to ensure their suspect didn't make a run for that way.

The detective flanked by six officers in tactical gear walked up to the door and knocked.

"Mr. Porter its Gates Point Police, we'd like a moment of your time."

There was movement inside and then the door open just a crack.

"How can I help you?"

"We'd like to ask you a few questions, may we come inside?"

"No."

"Mr. Porter we are looking for Eryn Upton and we have a warrant to search your premises, open the door."

"No!"

The door slammed shut.

The detective stepped back while the uniformed officers breached the front door of the house.

"Move in!" The detective called over the police radio.

The officers in the back of the house moved in from the park.

Rob Porter grabbed his laptop and was headed out a side window when he was grabbed by one of the officers in the house.

"Robert Porter you are under arrest."

Blue came in through the front door.

"Where is she?" He demanded.

"Who?"

Blue turned away, "Eryn!" He yelled.

"In here!"

Blue ran down the hallway. "Eryn, where are you?"

"Here"

He heard her voice from a room to his left. "Stand back!"

He kicked in the door.

Eryn was standing against the far wall with her hands on her hips. The sight of her made him smile.

"Eryn!" Blue rushed forward and swept her up in his arms.

Eryn wrapped her arms about his neck and buried her face in him.

They stood silent just holding each other each grateful for the other.

Blue finally broke the silence "I was so worried about you."

"I was starting to get a little worried, too." Eryn pulled away from him so she could see his face.

I was trying to find a way out through this window."

Blue smiled. "Good girl."

"I'm glad you came along when you did, though you know in case the window trick didn't work." She smiled.

"Come on let's get you checked out." He put his arm around her and led her out of the house.

Blue made her go to the hospital in the ambulance and have a thorough examination.

When she was done, Blue came in to check on her.

"Are you still here?" She asked surprised.

"Of course. Where else would I be?"

"At home getting some sleep." Eryn laughed, "You look a little tired."

"I'll sleep once I am confident you are okay and safely tucked in at home."

"Oh, I'm okay. He just locked me in a room is all. I barely saw him he spent all his time on the computer, ranting and mumbling."

"Well, you're safe now." Blue gave her a weak smile.

"Thank you." Eryn smiled sensing there was no point in arguing. If the chief of police wants to drive you home, it's probably a good idea to let him.

"I'll wait outside the door while you get dressed." He said and patted her arm.

Eryn dressed quickly anxious to be home and take a nice warm bath.

"All set." She announced when she opened the hospital room door.

"Good." Blue put his hand on her back and walked her outside to his SUV.

They drove in relative silence until they reached her house.

Blue got out and opened her door for her and walked her to the door.

"Well, I'm sure you want to get a good night's sleep." He said studying her features as if he was trying to memorize them.

"Well, yes, a hot bath and my bed do sound inviting right now, but I'm not in a rush if you want to come in for a minute." She thought he looked like a man with something on his mind.

"Just for a minute."

She nodded and unlocked the door, Blue closed it behind them and locked it.

"Wanna a beer or something?"

"I'd better not," Blue shuffled his feet a little and thumbed towards the door, "still gotta drive home."

Eryn nodded and decided to forgo her own beer. She thought she might want something stronger anyway.

"Listen Eryn," Blue stepped forward, "I need to tell you something and I am going to probably mess this up, but hear me out, okay?"

She nodded.

"I was really worried about you. I mean really worried. I thought," he paused and swallowed hard. "I thought I had lost you and I don't know what I would have done if you had been hurt or worse."

She watched his eyes flash as he spoke. She had a warm feeling building up in her chest.

"It made me realize how much I care about you." Blue took a step closer and framed her face gently with his hands. "I've never felt this way before and I don't want to lose you."

Eryn blinked and bit her lip.

"Eryn," he whispered. "I am in love with you, I love you more deeply than I have ever loved anyone."

Eryn's breath caught in her chest. She was a loss for words. She cared deeply for Blue, but she wasn't sure if she was ready to profess love.

"Blue,"

"I know this is a lot to take in right now, you've had a trying several days. But I just needed you to know."

He leaned for a kiss, and she let him. His lips were warm and gentle. The five o'clock stubble reminded her of his strength and ruggedly good looks. His tongue tentatively sought hers. She leaned into him, wrapping her arms around his neck, and letting her hands sink into his dark hair. She accepted his kiss moaned slightly when their tongues touched. The warm feeling in her chest began to spread quickly through the rest of her body. Blue's arms circled her like a steel cage, she could feel the strength of him as he held her, his hand cradling the back of her head. They broke away from one another breathless.

Blue rested his forehead against hers with his eyes closed.

"Eryn," he whispered.

"Hmmm?" She didn't trust herself to speak.

"I never want to let you go."

She smiled. She liked that idea, the doubts she had a few moments ago were fading quickly.

Blue opened his eyes to see Eryn staring up at him and smiling.

"I was so worried about you."

"I wasn't worried." She answered.

"You weren't?"

"No,"

"Why not?"

"Because I knew you would find me." She smiled.

"You did?"

Eryn nodded. "Yes."

He kissed her again, this time more deeply. Eryn knew she was going to lose herself in him, but she couldn't help it she let herself go and matched the passion if kiss.

Blue pulled himself away from her.

"Eryn," he panted.

"Yes, Blue."

"This feels like it is going somewhere, and as much as I really want to go there, I don't think it would be fair to you right now."

She felt disappointment and relief at the same time. She wanted more with Blue, but she hadn't had a shower, she was sure she looked a mess and probably didn't smell as fresh as she would like.

She giggled into the side of his neck a little.

"I probably do need a shower at least."

"Yeah, me too." He groaned.

She was torn, she wanted to invite him to stay and share the shower with her, but she also wanted to have a little alone time.

"I should go."

She wanted to say 'stay' but, she knew was right. So, she didn't say anything.

He took a step back from her and held her at arm's length.

"You are so beautiful."

She felt her cheeks blush. He kissed her on the forehead.

"I'm going to go and let you get some rest, but I am going to call you in the morning, and you might want to text Sarah and Penn."

"Oh yeah, you're right. I should."

He smiled down at her. He kissed her again.

Her body really didn't want him to leave.

"I'll call you in the morning." He said as he stepped back.

She bit her lip again, "Okay."

She followed him to the door.

"Make sure you lock up tight after I leave." He said as he leaned down to kiss her again.

"I will."

And he was gone. She closed the door and locked the deadbolt and the thumb lock. She wondered if that was enough. But Rob wasn't going to be coming back for her. Still, she felt a little nervous. She checked the windows, and the back door. Finally, she grabbed a bottle of wine and her cell phone and headed upstairs.

She ran a hot bath and then called Sarah and Penn on a group call.

"Eryn, is that you?" Sarah squealed.

"Hi, ladies. I just wanted to let you know I am home safe and sound."

"Oh my god, we were so worried!" Penn said.

"Tell us everything what happened, when did you get home?" Sarah asked.

"Do you want us to come over?" Penn added.

"I've got a bottle of wine and I am getting into the tub as we speak. So, no you don't need to come over."

"Well tell us everything!" Sarah said.

"Well, it was crazy, he was waiting for me in the shop and grabbed me from behind. He had something that knocked me out and then he had me locked in a room in his house."

"Oh my god!" Penn and Sarah exclaimed at once.

"Did he hurt you?" Penn asked.

"No, I really didn't see much of him, he was on his computer a lot."

"How did the police find you?" Penn asked.

Sarah cut in, "I can answer that, they figured out he had a fake social media account that he was using to stalk me with, and they traced the IP address back to his house." Sarah said. "Oh Eryn, I am so sorry, this is all my fault."

"How is it your fault?" Penn asked.

"Because he was using Eryn to get to me, the crazy bastard."

"Sarah, it was not your fault." Eryn reassured her.

"Yes, it is!" Sarah sniffed and Eryn knew she was crying.

"It totally was not, please don't think that. He was crazy as hell; you had no control of that."

"So, was Blue there?" Penn asked in a low suggestive tone.

"Yes, he was. He kicked in the door to the room where I was being held and then followed me to the hospital and then drove me home."

"Is he there now?" Penn asked.

"No," Eryn laughed. "You think I'd be calling you two if he was here and I was naked in a tub of water?"

"I hope to god, not!" Penn giggled.

"Okay, well I just wanted you guys to know I was okay. I'm going to soak, get drunk and go to bed."

"Okay, well don't worry about a thing, we've got the shop under control, you just take a couple of days to recuperate." Sarah said.

"I know you do." Eryn smiled "And I appreciate it very much."

They all clicked off. Eryn had no intention of taking any time off.

She sat in the tub until the water got cold, then she finished the bottle of wine, dried off and went to bed.

Her alarm went off at five and she was up and making coffee. She made breakfast and realized she was starving, then made a second helping of bacon and toast. Before getting dressed and heading out the door.

At seven her cell phone rang.

"Hello?"

"Eryn, you up?" Blue's voice greeted her.

"Yes, I'm up." She smiled and sat into her desk chair.

"Did you get any sleep?"

"I did actually. What about you? I hope your day isn't too busy."

"Oh, just the usual." Blue chuckled. "What about you?"

"Same, checking orders, stuff like that."

"Wait. Are you at work?" Blue asked.

"Of course, I'm at work."

"Eryn!" Blue scolded.

"What? I have a business to run, and I've been away along enough."

"I'm coming down there right now!" Blue clicked off before she could argue.

Eryn looked at her phone before putting it back in her pocket. She went to brew a pot of coffee in the small kitchenette. She had a feeling this was going to be a long day.

She walked up front to the retail area stopping at the spot where Rob had grabbed her. She couldn't help herself she looked over her shoulder just to make sure she was alone. She heard a vehicle come to an abrupt stop out front and knew it had to be Blue.

She strode to the double glass doors and opened one to see he is standing there with a scowl.

"Good morning." She smiled.

"What are you doing here?" He demanded.

"I told you I have a business to run, and I've already been out a couple of days."

"And the business is still here, and it didn't fall apart. You have great people working for you they can handle things for a few more days." Blue put his hands on her shoulders.

"But I'm fine."

"Eryn, you've been through a traumatic event, it's going to hit you and that is normal, but you need to take some time for yourself." Blue insisted.

"I'm okay. I mean, I am double checking the doors to make sure they are locked and everything."

"Well, I'm staying with you until someone else comes in." The look he gave didn't leave any more for argument.

"Well, then you better come in and have some coffee." She sighed.

He locked the door and followed her to the back.

She poured him a cup and offered him a seat at the small dinette table. "I'm really okay."

"You don't mind if I decide that for myself, do you?" He asked.

"No, I suppose not." She shook her head and reached for his hand. "Did you get some sleep last night?"

"A little."

"Maybe, you're the one that needs a day off." Eryn suggested.

"I won't argue with that." He got a devilish look in his eye, "Why don't we both take off, we can go somewhere on the boat for the weekend."

Eryn had to admit that sounded like a wonderful idea.

"I will if you will." She said.

"Really?" Blue perked up.

"Sure, you take a couple of days off and so will I."

"You're on!" He pointed in her direction and laughed.

They were laughing when Sarah came in.

"Hello?" She called out.

"In the kitchen!" Eryn called out.

"Eryn?" Sarah poked her head around the corner. "What the? What are you doing here?" She demanded.

"Getting back to work." Eryn said as if it was the most natural thing to come to work the day after you were rescued from a locked room after being kidnapped.

"You should be at home resting or," Sarah was nearly speechless, "or something."

"You're a bad influence on her," Eryn looked at Blue. "Everyone, please I'm fine. What good will come of me sitting at home in my bathrobe?"

"You can give yourself a chance to come to terms with what happened to you." Blue said repeating his previous concerns.

"But nothing happened to me, I wasn't harmed, I wasn't abused. He locked me in a room while he played on his computer."

"Weren't you scared?" Sarah asked.

"No, I knew Blue would come for me, it was a question of whether I'd find my own way out before he got there."

"Well, I need a day off to recover from the trauma of having my psycho ex-non-boyfriend kidnap my boss." Sarah looked devastated.

"Oh Sarah, it is not your fault at all. There is nothing for you to worry about. If you need the day, go ahead. It is okay. You deserve a day for keeping things running so smoothly while I was gone."

Sarah looked like she wanted to say yes but was afraid to.

"Seriously, Sarah, go home. Get some sleep, I won't take no for an answer." Eryn insisted.

Blue knew there was no point in arguing anymore with Eryn, so he turned to Sarah instead.

"Come on I'll drive you home."

"But, my car," Sarah started to protest.

"We'll take care of that later, leave the keys with Eryn."

Reluctantly Sarah left with Blue.

Eryn breathed a sigh of relief. She didn't want anyone spending the day fussing over her.

An hour later Penn arrived.

"Oh, there you are, I knew I'd find you digging in the dirt somewhere." Penn called as she came into the greenhouse.

Eryn stood and wiped her brow with the back of her forearm.

"Hi, Penn."

"Well, you don't look worse for wear, are you okay?"

"I'm fine."

"Well, I knew you would be, you are a tough bird."

"Thank you, I knew you would understand. I sent Sarah home; I just couldn't stand it if she was fussing over me all day."

"And Blue?"

"Thankfully, he has work to do that is more important than me or he'd be right here trying to carry things for me or something."

Penn smiled. "There are worse things."

"Yeah, I know but I can't think of any of them right now."

Penn laughed.

"Okay, well I've got to get to work myself. But call me later if you want to have a drink after work and forget your troubles."

"I just might do that." Eryn smiled grateful for Penn's understanding non-fussy way.

Chapter Thirteen

B lue sat at the bar talking to Chuck after work. It was late but he wasn't ready to go home.

"Man, what are you doing here? Why aren't you with Eryn?" Chuck admonished.

"She doesn't need me, she is perfectly fine, like nothing ever happened. I was trying to give her some space you know. Hoping she would get some rest or something."

"She at home?" Chuck asked.

"Yeah, she said she was headed home after work. I asked her if she wanted some company, but she said no."

"Maybe she is dealing with it in her own way and you babysitting her doesn't help. She's a pretty independent person."

"Yeah, I know. But I feel like I'm sitting around doing nothing. I mean, what if it hits her all at once and she realizes what a dangerous situation it actually was and what could have happened and I'm not there for her."

"First, of all, I think Eryn is probably aware of the situation and she also doesn't seem the type to worry about what might have happened. Bottom line, you were the knight in shining armor you saved her, and life goes on." Chuck wiped the counter as he spoke his wisdom from behind the bar.

"She doesn't need me." Blue finished his beer and put the glass down for another.

"Yes, she does, but not to be a babysitter, she needs you to be there for her when there are things she can't handle when she needs it, not when you need it." Chuck poured Blue another beer.

Blue just stared at him.

"I just thought after this was over. . .,"

"You thought she'd fall into your arms, and she swoon or something?" Chuck had to try hard not to laugh a little. "What's gotten into you?"

"She has gotten to me. She makes me want to rescue her and whisk her away someplace safe. To protect her from the world." Blue downed half his beer in one gulp.

Chuck couldn't help himself anymore and started to laugh.

"What's so funny?" Blue demanded.

"You man, you have some very old-fashioned ideas and I'm afraid that woman you're in love with is anything but old fashioned."

"Yeah," Blue was starting to feel the effects of two pints of beer on an empty stomach.

"Come on, before someone sees the chief of police passed out in a bar." Chuck came out from behind the bar and led Blue to his office in the back. Blue stretched out on the sofa. While Chuck went back to close the restaurant.

"Why are you out with Blue tonight?" Penn asked as she poured another glass of wine for herself.

"Because I felt like he would spend the whole date asking me how I felt or something. I don't need that."

"Are you sure?" Penn looked at her.

"Yes, why wouldn't I be."

"So why don't you want him asking if you are alright. I'd love to have a man ready to wait on me hand and foot." Penn smiled wickedly.

"Because I don't need a man hovering over me." Eryn sniped.

"Why the hell not?"

"Because." Eryn took on a petulant look.

"Are you kidding me? Girl, how long have we known each other?" Penn sat up straight.

"A while." Eryn mumbled.

"What has happened during all that time that you suddenly don't want the company of a good man?"

"Maybe the realization that there aren't any?" Eryn replied.

"Do you believe Blue is not a good man?"

Eryn stared at her wine hating it when Penn was right.

"I believe Blue is a good man."

"With only the best intentions?" Penn prodded.

"Maybe."

"Okay, well you better call that man and tell him you need him to come over here." Penn picked up Eryn's cell phone off the table and tossed it to her.

"Fine." Eryn said sticking her tongue out at Penn which only made Penn giggle. Blue's voicemail picked up.

"Blue, it's Eryn. I was wondering, well I know it's late, but I was wondering if you could come over?"

She had to admit she was disappointed that he didn't answer. She was starting to feel like a heel.

"No answer?" Penn asked.

Eryn shook her head no.

"Well, maybe he is working late." Penn tried to sound hopeful.

"Or maybe I was too much of a jerk and he decided he didn't have time for someone like me."

"Are you serious? Wow, it must be the wine, you are swinging left and right, tonight." Penn reached over and moved the wine bottle away from Eryn.

"Come on let's watch a movie or something." Eryn picked up the remote and moved to sit next to Penn on the sofa.

"Okay, popcorn?" Penn asked getting up and heading to Eryn's kitchen.

"Yes, I'll find a nice movie while you make the popcorn, with extra butter!" Eryn called after her.

Penn left in the wee hours of the morning complaining she would have bags under her eyes and Saturday was the busiest day at her boutique.

Eryn decided she would take Sarah's advice and take Saturday off. She sent text messages to the Saturday crew and was met with assurances that she should take a couple of days and they would be happy to handle things.

"Maybe a day or two off wasn't such a bad idea after all. She had never heard from Blue and was a little disappointed. Perhaps she had pushed him away too hard. She would only have herself to blame for that. It made her want to cry more than being kidnapped and locked in a room. She started to make coffee and then decided she didn't want any and she went and curled up on the sofa and closed her eyes in hopes she could go back to sleep and forget all of it.

Blue woke up on the sofa of Chuck's office. His neck and back were stiff. It was not like crashing on a friend's sofa when he was in his twenties that was for sure. He stood up and looked around. He didn't see any signs of Chuck. He checked his pockets for his cell phone and saw that he had a voice mail. He pressed the button and listen to Eryn's voice as she asked him to come over last night. He checked the time. She was probably already on her way to work. He rushed out of the office and was greeted by one of the cooks.

"Chuck said to make you some breakfast if you wanted it."

"No, thank you. I have to go. But thanks anyway." Blue rushed out of restaurant to his car. He peeled out of the parking lot and raced to the nursery. He felt like such a jerk. Eryn had called needing him, wanting his company and he had been drunk. He really needed to get right and get to her. He imagined her being alone and needing someone and there wasn't anyone. He blew through a yellow light and swung into the parking lot. He didn't see her car. He started to have a sinking feeling in the pit of his stomach. He walked to the retail shop doors, and they were locked. He headed for the green houses and slipped in.

"Hello?"

A young man popped up from a row of plants.

"Can I help you?"

"Police Chief Keegan, is Eryn here?"

"No, she isn't coming in today. Sent a text said she was taking the day off."

"Did she say if she was sick or anything?"

"No, didn't say."

"Thank you." Blue raced back out to the parking lot and headed for Eryn's house. He was really concerned now. Eryn not going to work was serious business. Things may have been worse than he thought, and he had left her to deal with it on her own. He would never forgive himself.

He screeched to a halt in front of her house and ran to the door.

He rang the bell then knocked. "Eryn? You home?"

The locks clicked and then the door opened. Eryn stood in front of him her hair was a complete mess, she was wearing a huge thick bathrobe and a pair of socks. He smiled despite himself.

"Hey." He whispered.

"Hey, what are you doing here? Shouldn't you be at work or something?" Eryn blinked up at him still sleepy.

"I have something more important to do today," he studied her, "can I come in?"

"Oh sure." Eryn stepped aside.

Blue stepped inside and waited for her to close and relock the door.

"Eryn, I am so sorry. I feel like the biggest jerk in the world right now, and I wouldn't blame you if you didn't ever want to see me again." He blurted out.

Eryn stared at him for a moment and then the stress of the past several days bubbled to the top all at once and she let out a sob.

Blue wrapped his arms around her and held her tightly. He put his chin on top of her head effectively enveloping her in with his body. He stroked her head and let her cry. He knew it was coming and he was glad she was finally letting it out.

"That's right, let it all out." He whispered.

Eryn cried until her body was wracked with sobs.

"Come on, let's go sit down." He loosened his arms enough to let her walk with me to the sofa. He noticed the popcorn bowl and the empty wine bottles. Here were still two glasses on the table, one with lipstick so he knew Penn must have been here at some point.

They sat down and Eryn snuggled up against him. He pulled the blanket that was bunched up at the end of the sofa up around her and then held her as close as he could. She sniffled and sobbed some more, but the tears had stopped at least for now.

"I'm so sorry, Eryn." Blue said again, not sure what else to say.

"Why?" Eryn hiccupped.

"Because I wasn't here for you when you called last night."

"You have to work, I understand that."

"But I wasn't at work." He had to tell her the truth.

Eryn leaned up so she could look up into his face.

"I was passed out drunk at Chuck's place, feeling sorry for myself because I thought you didn't need me," He looked down at her and hated himself even more. "It was a selfish thing to do, and I hate myself."

Eryn reached up slowly and stroked his cheek. It was rough from not being shaved. He must have come straight from Chuck's, she thought.

"You don't have to apologize to me." She said her lips brushing his ears.

"Yes, I do. I'm a fool. I should have stayed with you no matter what."

"But I told you I was fine, and you respected my wishes. What more could you do?"

"I could have camped out on your doorstep. Or I could have answered my damn phone. It won't happen again, Eryn. I promise you that."

"Oh Blue," she wanted to say more but he covered her mouth with his drowning out the words.

"Now, you are sure he didn't hurt you in anyway?" Blue asked once they had broken their kiss.

"Yes, I'm sure."

"You'd tell me, wouldn't you?" Blue looked down at her. He had witnessed too many women who had been assaulted that wouldn't or couldn't tell their loved ones what had happened to them.

"Yes, I promise I would tell you."

"Okay." Blue was satisfied with her answer and pulled her close to his chest once again. He knew that sometimes talking was overrated and a hug was the best medicine. He hoped he was doing the right thing for Eryn. He wanted her to trust him, to understand that he would never let his guard down again and he would protect her.

Eryn fell asleep against Blue's chest. It was the best sleep she remembered having in a very long time.

Chapter Fourteen

"I think we should have a party." Penn announced at lunch.

Sarah and Eryn looked at her forks paused in mid-air.

"What are we celebrating?" Eryn asked.

"You being returned safe and sound and Sarah being free of her unbalanced stalker." Penn said cheerfully.

Sarah looked a little dubious at the idea. "Are you sure a party is appropriate?" She asked.

"Why not?"

"Well, I've just never heard of a party to celebrate your new boss surviving being kidnapped by a guy one dated briefly." Sarah said before taking a bite of her salad.

"Sarah, please. You know I don't want you to feel bad about this whole affair. You are just as much as victim as I was. I don't blame you in the slightest. It is not at all your fault. And I agree, I'm not sure what to wear to a stalker free party." She eyed Penn.

"Well, you two are just a couple of party poopers." Penn huffed.

"Look Penn, I know how you love to have a party, but can we have it for a different reason, I don't think we should give this guy Rob any more attention than he has already gotten." Eryn suggested.

"Well, you do have a point there." Penn agreed. "What should we celebrate?" She looked between Eryn and Sarah.

The girls laughed. "Well, we better come up with a theme if she is determined to have a party." Eryn said to Sarah.

"I guess so."

"What about, a party to celebrate Eryn finally taking a day off." Sarah joked.

"Or a party to celebrate Eryn finally has a boyfriend." Penn joined in the fun.

"How a party to celebrate something that doesn't have anything to do with me." Eryn suggested.

"Well, we could celebrate Sarah passing her probationary period at work." Penn thought out loud.

"She wasn't on probation. Eryn clarified.

"Oh," Penn looked at her soup as if it would offer her a suggestion. "Then what about a friendship party, one to celebrate old and new friends."

"Now, that idea I like." Eryn agreed and looked to Sarah.

"A friendship party," she seemed to be testing the words. "Yes, I think that theme would work. Where should we have it?"

"Well, I know a guy with a restaurant." Eryn suggested.

"You seem to know a lot of guys to be so tragically single." Penn observed.

"Look who is talking!" Eryn laughed.

"When do we want to have this party?" Sarah asked.

"Well, I don't know. I supposed soon, but it might depend on the availability of the venue." Eryn advised.

"Okay, can you get with this friend of yours and find out if he has any availability?" Penn took out a notepad and began jotting down the details.

"I can, but do we have an idea of how many people we are talking here? That will help with the availability, like will we need a banquet room or the whole restaurant."

"Hmm, we'll the three of us, of course," Penn began ticking off numbers of people. "We each should have a plus one."

"I won't have a plus one." Sarah said sadly.

"Well, you can have one if you want, I can set you up with someone I know." Penn offered cheerily.

"I'm not sure I'm ready to date just now."

"Penn leave her alone. She will find her own date when and if she wants one." Eryn admonished.

Sarah smiled at Eryn gratefully. Despite Eryn's insistence that the whole kidnapping affair was not her fault, she couldn't help but feel like it was. She had terrible taste in men. Rob was an extreme example. But she hadn't had a relationship that lasted more than six months since college. And she didn't really have the interesting in dating anymore. It just didn't seem worth it.

Eryn had Blue, which was nice, and Penn never seemed to have any trouble getting a date, but Sarah thought that was because of her success in the fashion industry and just the sheer volume of people Penn knew. Sarah pushed her salad around on her plate she suddenly was no longer hungry.

"Okay, well why don't we say twenty people as a round number for starters." Penn said closing the notepad.

"Okay, I will call Chuck and see what we can do." Eryn said hoping to close the matter. "Sarah and I need to get back to work." Eryn smiled at Sarah she could see the topic made her uncomfortable.

"Okay, well you two go on I'll get the check." Penn waived them away.

"Okay, I'll get it next time." Eryn offered.

"Yes, you will." Penn laughed.

Eryn drove back to the nursery. "You know Penn is just trying to help the only way she knows how." Eryn said to Sarah.

"I know, and I know you are okay with the situation. But I'm not. I still feel guilty, no matter what you say, and I don't know how to shake that feeling." Sarah offered Eryn a weak smile.

"Have you spoken to anyone about this, I mean like a counselor or someone?"

"No."

"Maybe you should. I think it might help and there is really nothing for you to feel guilty about." Eryn tried to sound reassuring. "if you feel guilty that is Rob winning from jail. He still has some influence over you, and you are stronger than that." Eryn said. "Don't let him win, Sarah. Talk to someone."

"Okay. I will."

"I mean it. There is a number at the office for a counselor that is covered by our health insurance. Call, make an appointment. I think you can even do a video chat if you feel more comfortable doing that." Eryn offered.

"I will call, I promise."

"Okay, good." Eryn smiled. "Now, we need to concentrate on next week's orders."

Sarah smiled. Work helped keep her mind off of things. It was the one thing she still felt like she could control and right now she needed to be in control of something.

"Of course, you can have a party here, Eryn." Chuck said into the phone. "When do you want to have it?"

"Well, we left that sort of up in the air depending on your availability."

"Okay, we'll let me see."

Eryn could hear him tapping on the keyboard.

"Will two weeks give you enough time to work out the rest of the details?" Chuck asked.

"Yes, I believe it would."

"Okay, I'll put you down for March 23rd. How about that?"

"That sounds perfect, Chuck. Thank you."

Eryn clicked off with a date set, it would give Penn something to work with as far as invitations and she would let Penn handle the menu directly with Chuck.

Work was booming with the promise of spring only a month and a half away she wasn't going to have a lot of free time to devote to party planning. She was also scheduling weekend gardening classes as people started preparing to start their gardens.

She wanted to see more of Blue, but it was difficult with the extra hours unloading trucks after closing and scheduling classes. She was trying to work out a schedule the greenhouse staff to teach the classes so that she could take more weekends off to spend with Blue cruising the Chesapeake Bay.

And now there was Penn and the friendship party.

"I can't believe you are doing this to me!" Penn cried.

"What? You can do this, for god's sake you plan entire fashion shows. You can handle twenty people for dinner at a restaurant." Eryn snapped.

"I know but that is not the point. I need you for morale support!" Penn insisted.

"You have Sarah." Eryn nodded in Sarah's direction.

"I know, and she is amazing, but three heads are better than two, no offense." Penn looked at Sarah who was stifling a giggle.

"None taken."

"Look you have been harping on me to take some time off for years, and you have been harping on me to find a boyfriend. So now I have a boyfriend who I am going to take some time off to be with for a week, you should be ecstatic I finally took your advice. This is the "I told you so" opportunity of the decade!" Eryn sorted through the clothes she had laid out on her bed in prepared for her trip with Blue.

"Who cruises the bay this time of year for Pete's sake, the water is still freezing, and the weather is completely unpredictable." Penn threw up her hands.

"I know that is what makes it exciting." Eryn argued.

"You hate the cold!" Penn continued.

"What makes you think I will be cold?" Eryn gave her a devious grin.

Sarah giggled out loud.

"I give up!" Penn stormed out of the room.

Sarah looked after her.

"Don't worry about her she is just having a drama queen moment; she'll get over it."

"She does have a point; February can be a little iffy when it comes to the weather."

"I know, but it was the only time both Blue and I could get off from work and we didn't want to wait until summer." Eryn explained.

"I understand that part, but why not go in a car and stay somewhere with a warm fireplace or something." Sarah suggested. It was a very reasonable idea, and the cabin rental rates were good this time of year, the prices didn't go up until mid-April.

"Because there isn't much to see inside a cabin." Eryn explained.

"And you really plan to spend time topside?" Sarah said in a low suggestive tone.

"It's amazing what you can do under the stars." Eryn laughed.

"Well, I for one, am glad you are going regardless." Sarah picked up a long sleeve thermal shirt and began folding it.

"Thank you."

A moment later Penn was back, she walked over to the bed and began inspecting the wardrobe choices.

"Well, if you insist on going at least let me help you with your packing." Penn said with a heavy sigh.

Eryn winked at Sarah behind Penn's back and nodded.

"Would you?" Eryn played to Penn's hand.

"Don't patronize me!" Penn fussed.

The next Saturday, Blue and Eryn drove to the marina to leave on their one-week cruise up to St. Michael, Maryland.

"Are you sure you are okay with this?" Blue asked Eryn for the one hundredth time.

"Of course, why wouldn't I be?"

"I don't know, too soon. Will you feel too confined on the boat?"

"No," She looked at him as if he had grown a third eye on his forehead. "That is ridiculous."

"You know, I forget how tough you are sometimes." Blue shook his head smiling.

"Is it a problem, do you prefer damsels in distress?"

"Hell no."

"Okay, let's finish loading up the gear and head out." She said, not wanting to talk about it anymore.

"Yes, ma'am." Blue smiled and carried a bag of groceries aboard.

Eryn's stretched and took a deep breath. She loved the smell of salt air, nothing like low tide to make her feel like she was home. She couldn't imagine living anywhere that wasn't near the salt marshes, the bay and the rivers that fed it. The plant life around the water's edge was fascinating and the wildlife was beautiful. She often would close her eyes and try to imagine what it was like along these shores before the influx of human population began to delete the resources and pollute the waters. It was such a shame.

"All set." Blue called to her.

"Permission to come aboard." She asked.

"Come ahead." Blue held up a hand to assist her, not that she needed it, but it was the polite thing to do and no matter how independent she was, he would not forget his manners. She could refuse him if she wanted to, but he was still always going to offer her a hand, an elbow or his assistance in some form or fashion.

It took an hour to get everything stowed away and by then the tide was starting to come in. They sat at the table and looked over their route again. Predicting when they would arrive at various points along the way. They planned to explore inlets and creeks stopping at small towns. Eryn was excited, but it was going to be cold, but she had a feeling they would find a way to stay warm. She was hoping it would snow during the trip she thought being on the Chesapeake Bay while it snowed would be just a beautiful as a sunset in the summertime.

Chapter Fifteen

It didn't take long for Eryn to remember her crewing skills from her days wondering the planet with Penn. Blue was a good teacher and the boat being more modern and could steer itself, not that Blue would allow that to happen. He cherished his boat and wouldn't take any unnecessary risks.

Eryn was glad they could pilot it from inside rather than exposed on the deck. Blue had the weather radio on as well as the radar when she joined him and brought him a mug of coffee.

"Thank you," he took the mug and appraised her up and down. "You warm enough?"

"I'm fine," she said standing next to him and looking out ahead. "This is really amazing. I feel relaxed already."

He smiled at her happy that she had agreed to come on this adventure with him and glad she was away from work, and he was happy to have her all to himself. "I'm glad you're here."

They traveled for a while in silence, Blue watching the radar and keeping an eye out for larger vessels while Eryn scanned the horizon looking for wildlife, the sky was cloudless, and the winds were fair, and it was a perfect day. Once they were free of the shipping channels Blue stayed as close to shore as the water depth would allow. There Eryn watched gulls and ducks all looking for a meal.

Blue looked over at her, "Are you doing, okay?"

"Sure, what about you? No regrets?"

"Regrets?" He was puzzled.

"Yeah, no separation anxiety from work or your cell phone?"

He laughed, "No, but what about you?"

"I'd lie if I didn't say I didn't wonder how things were going back at the nursey, but it's like you said I have a good crew and I trust them so nothing for me to worry about." She gave him a tight smile. While she did feel more relaxed, she couldn't stop her mind from wondering back to work.

"What about the trial, you sure you going to be okay with that?"

"Oh yeah, but we have time to worry about that," she waved him off, that isn't until April and there are plenty of things to do before then."

"I know but I just want you to be prepared it isn't like it is on TV when you're the one being questions and grilled. It is easy to forget things or to feel an enormous amount of pressure."

"I'll be fine, you'll be there won't you?"

"Of course,"

"And the case against Rob is airtight, right?"

"We have all of his files fromm his computer the messages to Sarah and the tracking device we found on her car with his fingerprints all over it. It is kinda hard to believe that his attorney even has an argument to make."

"It is all sad in a way, his whole life ruined."

"Well, his defense is diminished capacity, I don't agree with that totally because he is very intelligent, but he has a disconnect with reality for sure and he does need help."

"I'm more worried about Sarah and what this will do to her to relive all of this again. And I hope he gets help to break this so-called connection he thinks he has with her. I don't want to think about her having to look over her shoulder all the time wondering if this guy is coming after her again."

"Well, hopefully he will be away for a long time getting some help and Sarah will be able to move on, but it will be hard on her during the trial. She is lucky to have friends like you and Penn."

"Well, like me anyway, I don't know about Penn." Eryn laughed.

Blue laughed, "Penn takes getting to know but in her own way she cares about you and I'm sure Sarah very much."

"I hope she wasn't too much of a pain the neck while I was missing."

"She kept us all on track and focused."

"That is a very objective view of the situation."

Blue shrugged, "We were all worried, but that is behind for now and I think we should just focus on this week, what do you think?" He said pulling her close.

She giggled and wrapped her arms around his neck and kissed him lightly. "I totally agree."

"You know we haven't really discussed the sleeping arrangements." Blue said nuzzling her neck.

"Oh, I didn't think we needed to discuss that." She whispered in his ear.

Blue held her at arm's length to look into her eyes. "Are you serious?"

She smiled at him deviously. "Yeah, I thought we would take turns standing watch." She giggled at the look of shear disappointment on his face.

"Oh, you are funny!" He laughed. He maneuvered her off his lap and steered the boat into an inlet and dropped the anchor.

Eryn looked at him confused, "What are you doing?"

"Making a point." He stood up and scooped her into his arms and carried her below to the stateroom and laid her down on the bed.

Eryn's heart was racing as he hovered over her.

Blue smiled at her and began kissing her intently. She responded letting go of her inhibitions for once. Blue's hands were roaming her body, but they stayed on the outside of her clothes. When he stopped, she opened her eyes and looked up at him.

"I am ready when you are, but only when you are." He kissed her nose. "Now we need to get dinner started, we wouldn't want to miss our first sunset." He stood up smiling at her.

Eryn was trying to catch her breath she was ready, but she could play hard to get too. She tucked her hair behind her ears and slid off the end of the bed.

"You're absolutely right, I don't want to miss a single sunset." She had called his bluff and she grinned to herself as he followed her to the galley.

"Do we have anything for dinner, or do you need to catch something?" She asked trying to keep him off balance.

"We are having spaghetti tonight." He said as he began to gather the ingredients and the large pot.

"What can I do to help?"

"Just keep me company." He pointed to a chair.

"Okay." She sat down and watched him. She admired the way he filled out his jeans and the thick sweater he was wearing. He knew his way around the galley

She helped him set the table and then closed her eyes after taking her first bite of spaghetti, "where did you learn to cook so well?"

"Ah, years of practice," he smiled her her. "I'm glad you like it."

"This is really delicious. Did Chuck teach you how to cook?"

Blue laughed. It was nice to hear him really laugh for a change.

"Absolutely not. No years of bachelorhood was my teacher, it was learn or starve."

She didn't know much about any of his previous relationships and she never quite knew when or how to ask. Finally, she had decided it didn't matter.

"Well, all that practice paid off." She smiled taking another bite

"Yes, it did." He said staring at her and smile playing at the corners of his mouth.

Chapter Sixteen

Sarah had developed a new appreciation for Eryn, it has been one thing to keep things going while Eryn had been kidnapped but, she had been distracted then. Now she was concentrating on all the details of the day to day for the business and the retail side of things and she was exhausted She didn't know how Eryn did it, and she wasn't even dealing with the landscaping schedule or the greenhouses. Rick was handling all of that whis week. Her phone buzzed for what seemed like the one hundredth time,

"Hello?"

"Sarah, it's Penn."

"Hi, Penn."

"Listen are can you do me a huge favor this evening? I was supposed to go to the restaurant and talk to the chef about the menu for our party, but I just got a call from a client who is in town and wants to stop by the shop for a private showing."

"Uh, I guess so, I've never had to plan a menu for a party before, do you have something in mind or a price range?"

"Yes, I'll email it to you, you're a gem. I really appreciate it."

"Good luck with the showing."

Sarah clicked off and waited for the email. A few minutes later she had it. Then she looked up the Seabreeze on the internet to get the address and directions. After work she drove down to the waterfront and found the Seabreeze at the end of the street.

The parking lot was starting to fill up and three other cars pulled in at the same time she did.

The hostess greeted her, "How many in your party this evening."

"Oh, no sorry I'm here to discuss party menu with the chef. I believe we had an appointment."

"Sure, what's your name?"

"Sarah."

"Okay, do you mind waiting in the bar and I'll have Chef come up and get you."

"No problem, thanks." Sarah stepped into the bar she wasn't sure what she was supposed to do. She didn't want to take up a table and she didn't really feel comfortable sitting alone at the bar and giving the wrong impression. So, she stood awkwardly to the side. More people came and took tables or barstools, she felt like she was getting lost in the crowd and she wondered if the chef would even see here standing in the corner. She looked around nervously.

"Sarah?"

She looked up at a very large man in whites looking down at her with incredible green eyes.

"Uh, I'm Sarah." She stammered.

A big grin spread across his face as he held out his hand. "I'm Chuck, come on let's go someplace quiet."

She looked around the room again, she hoped Chuck was also the chef. She followed him through the crowded bar and through the kitchen.

"Be careful, watch herself." He cautioned as he guided her past hot stoves, weaving through kitchen staff to an office.

"You're here about the party right, with Eryn?"

"Yes, Penn was supposed to meet with you tonight, but she got caught up at work and asked if I would come instead."

He smiled an easy smile. "No problem, you work with Eryn, right?"

"Yes," she wasn't sure if she would be flattered or mortified that Eryn may have been talking about her. "How do you know Eryn?"

"Sit," He motioned to a chair, "I met her through Blue, he and I go way back."

"Oh," now it all made sense. She had wondered how Eryn knew this guy and had assumed that it was through the Chamber or something similar. But know he was a friend of Blue's made things click into place.

"Would you like something to drink?" Chuck offered.

"No, thank you. I'm fine." She sat ramrod straight in the chair, ready to do business.

"Okay, so I understand you guys want to have a party, is it casual? Is there a theme I need to work with?"

Sarah took a deep breath, how was she going to explain this party to a perfect stranger.

"Well, the party was Penn's idea, do you know Penn?"

He shook his head, "No."

"Oh, okay well. Penn likes to have parties for no reason at all, well there is always a motive I suppose because it usually turns into a way for her to market her clothing, but this is supposed to be just a friendship party."

Chuck sat watching her a smile playing at the corner of his lips. "This Penn sounds like an interesting person."

"Oh, she is definitely that."

Chuck grinned.

"I mean, she is sweet and would do anything in the world to help a friend. That is actually what started the idea for the party she wanted to do something nice for Eryn after she was kidnapped." Sarah bit her tongue she didn't know if Chuck knew about the kidnapping, and she didn't want to have to explain her part in it.

"Yes, I can understand that, how is Eryn doing? I know Blue was a mess until they found her."

"She seems to be doing just fine, she and Blue are cruising the bay right now, which is why Penn, and I are handling the arrangements and not Eryn."

"But if the party was supposed to be in honor of Eryn, why would she be making the arrangements?"

"Because, Penn is great at ideas, not so great at execution and Eryn will take over rather than see something done halfway. And besides Eryn talked her out of a party in her honor and said it should just be about friendship in general if there had to be a party, which Eryn doesn't really want."

"All of that, huh?" Chuck was smiling at her.

"Oh no! I've said too much. I'm so sorry." Eryn felt her face redden as she realized she had been prattling on nervously.

"Well, I'm glad Blue and Eryn are out of town and someone else is handling the party, Eryn seems like she already has a lot on her plate, but I'm sorry it got dumped in your lap."

"Oh, I don't mind really. Especially if it helps Eryn, but the problem is I've never done this sort of thing before so I'm not really sure what to do." She pulled out her phone and pulled up Penn's email. "Penn did send me a list of ideas she wanted to run past you."

"Okay, that sounds like a great place to start, can you forward that list to me?"

Sarah nodded and typed in his email as he recited it to her. Then she heard a chime on his computer indicating he had received her email.

Chuck looked over Penn's list. "Your friend has some pretty expensive tastes."

Sarah sighed, "I was afraid of that, listen I'm not sure who is paying for this, if Eryn is paying for part of it or what, and I want to be fair to you and your staff for your time and efforts but if there is anyway...." She blushed.

Chuck heled up his hand, "Don't worry about a thing, I'll make it work and give you a fair price, deal?"

He held out his hand. Sarah stood up and shook it. "Deal."

"Now, do you want to sample some of our dishes, so you know what you are paying for?"

"Oh, I don't want to take up any more of your time."

"You really haven't done this before have you?"

Sarah wasn't sure if she was more embarrassed at her inexperience, or the fact that she couldn't stop staring his eyes.

"I, uh,"

Chuck gave her a reassuring smile. "Have a seat, it is part of what I am going to charge you for so you might as well enjoy it. I'll be right back."

Sarah stood looking around after he had left not sure what to do. She was pulled to a group of pictures on the wall of soldiers. She had to look closely to realize that two of the men in the photo were Chuck and Blue.

"Okay, we are all set, come with me." He gave her a warm smile and noticed the picture she was examining.

"You have known Blue a long time haven't you?" She said as they walked back through the kitchen and into an empty dining room.

"I look that old do I?"

"Oh no! I didn't mean that at all!" Sarah spun around to face him and almost tripped. Chuck reached out and steadied her.

"I was only joking, no worries, love." He guided her down into a chair.

Sarah wanted nothing more but to get up and run out of the place, but she wasn't sure which way it was to the exit, and she would probably only crash into something along the way.

Two of the waitstaff came out carrying trays loaded with food.

Sarah looked at Chuck, "What is all of this?"

"Well, it isn't everything you friend asked for but it is samples of our more popular dishes and so you can taste each one and tell me what you think." Chuck nodded to the staff, and they disappeared.

"This is way too much."

"Well how can you know what you like the best if you haven't tried everything."

"There goes my diet for next six months."

Chuck ignored the comment and brought over a cup of soup. "She-crab, is my personal favorite." He sat it down in front of her.

She picked up the spoon and tried a little bit. "Yes, that is delicious. But I'm not sure soup is going to translate well in a party setting."

"You may have a point." Chuck frowned and looked at the other items on the tray. "Ah! Crab puff, you'll love these." He put one down in front of her on a small plate.

"Hmm, that is wonderful!"

"Excellent. I'll put crab puffs on the menu. So how long as you worked for Eryn?"

"A few months now."

"Here try this." He pushed a bacon wrapped scallop towards her.

"Hmm, this is delicious, but I'm concerned about the pork factor."

"Pork factor?" He stopped and looked at her.

"Not everyone eats pork, I mean it is okay to have this on the menu as long as we have a comparable option."

He smiled broadly, "I see your point, cheese straw?"

"Um, okay."

"With or without dip?"

She tasted the cheese straw. "It is good without, what sort of dip did you have in mind?"

"Mariana?"

"That could work, now aren't going heavy on the seafood. What if there is a shellfish allergy?"

"You have a point."

"Try this wine, for those having seafood, it is our house white, but see if you think it is up to your friend's standards."

She took a sip and then another. "Hmm its good but not sure Penn is going to like it; she prefers them a little drier than that."

"Okay what about this one?" He handed her a glass of Stags Leap.

"Yes, that is more like it."

"I have some chicken items as well, want to try those while we are sampling the white wines?"

"Sure."

They spent another hour going over the chicken, beef, and dessert items we well as red and dessert wines.

"Well, you may not have a lot of experience at party planning, but I think you did a fabulous job." Chuck leaned back and smiled at her. What is it that you do for Eryn?"

Sarah smiled she was feeling a little tipsy from the wine tasting.

"I'm a bookkeeper."

"Well, if you ever want to do something different you are welcome to come work for me in the catering division."

Sarah giggled, "I don't know anything about catering. Well, you just schooled me on this menu, and you know about budgeting a party, so I think you know more than you give yourself credit for."

Sarah looked at her watch, "Is that the time? Oh my gosh!"

"I'm sorry am I keeping you from a date?" Chuck looked truly repentant.

"A date, no." Sarah smiled. She stood up and wobbled a little.

"Maybe you better let me drive you home or call a cab or something that wine will sneak up on you."

"Oh, I didn't realize I had that much to drink. I really don't think I should drive. A cab will be fine I don't want to impose on you any further."

"Don't be ridiculous, any friend of Eryn or Blue's is a friend of mine. Give me just a minute." He disappeared and then returned without his apron and with a jacket.

"Come on, I'll drive you home." He steered Sarah out a side entrance to the restaurant and to his car parked out back.

He opened the car door and helped her inside. Sarah settled into the seat. Chuck slid in the passenger side and started the car.

"Where to?"

Sarah gave him the address and Chuck put the car in gear.

"Your car is very quiet." Sarah noticed.

"Its electric so no moving parts."

"Oh, cool!"

"Yes, it is great, no engine repairs, or oil changes, no gas to pay for."

"Wow, that is smart." She started looking around at how roomy it was. She was going to have to investigate models that she might be able to afford.

Chuck pulled up in front of her apartment and walked her to the door.

"If you give me your car keys, I'll have your car dropped off by morning for you."

"I'm so sorry to cause you so much trouble."

"It's no trouble."

"It's okay, I'll have Penn drive me back to the restaurant in the morning to get it." Sarah wasn't entirely comfortable giving her keys to Chuck even if he was a friend of Blue's.

"Okay, it was nice meeting you and I still say you are one hell of a party planner."

"Thanks."

Chuck waited while she unlocked the door and heard it lock again from the inside before he walked back to his car. He paused and looked around before getting in and driving away.

Chapter Seventeen

E ryn and Blue spent the night sleeping in the cabin after falling asleep while watching the moon rise over the bay. The next working Eryn felt refreshed despite her stiff back.

She stood up and stretched and tiptoed out onto deck. The sun was just rising, and it was chilly. But it was peaceful, and she closed her eyes and breathed deeply. She felt Blue's arms snake around her midsection. They were like warm muscular ropes.

His lips brushed her ear.

"I don't think there is anything more beautiful than you and the sunrise."

She closed her eyes and leaned back into him.

"Eryn," he whispered. She turned to face him. He was staring deep into her eyes and she was reminded in that moment she was lost to him forever. It was like their heart started to beat as one. Her universe shifted slightly and seemed to click into place. Blue lifted her up in his arms and carried to the stateroom. This time there would be no hesitating, no stopping. He kissed her slowly and deeply. His hands moving across her body. Her hands began exploring him.

Three hours later Blue left the bed to retrieve bottled water for her. Eryn accepted the water and pulled Blue back down to her.

"I don't want this to end."

He smiled down at her, "Nothing says it has to."

"Let's stay here forever."

"Okay. You call Sarah and tell her you are putting her in charge, and I'll quit my job and we will just drift up and down the Bay."

"Mmmm, sounds perfect." She nuzzled his neck.

"Eryn?"

"Yes?"

"I love you more than anything, and those words aren't enough."

"I love you, Jeremy Keegan."

He grinned at the use of his full name. "I don't know your middle name." He declared.

"Elizabeth,"

"Eryn Elizabeth Upton, my heart wants to burst at the sight of you."

"What's your middle name?"

"Patrick."

"Jeremy Patrick Keegan, I can't imagine my life without you."

He slipped back under the covers and ran his hand down her stomach. "I need to feed you."

"Not yet." She rolled into him.

They finally pulled into St. Michaels, Maryland.

"Eryn, I need to run some errands ashore, do you want to meet me at the Old Brick Café in an hour and a half?"

"Um, sure."

"Great, come on." He helped from the boat to the pier.

Blue had been secretly doing some research on his phone and knew exactly what he wanted and were he needed to go. He made sure Eryn wasn't watching which direction he went as he headed to Talbot Street and Guilford & Company Fine Jewelry. He had seen a ring online and he was having the owner hold it for him. It was a beautiful two carat Edwardian and platinum ring that he knew Eryn would love. He didn't care what it cost him he wanted that ring for Eryn.

With the ring purchased, he headed to the Kemp House and made a reservation for the night. Then he found Eryn sipping coffee out on the terrace in sunshine admiring some flowers.

"Hey, there you are." He smiled giving her a peck on the cheek.

"Hi, there. Where did you go?"

"Oh, just working on a little surprise for you."

Eryn giggled, "Really?"

"Yes, but you have to wait just a little while." He laughed. "What are you doing?"

"Just admiring the primroses."

"Is that what they are?" He looked at the beds and large urns full small colorful flowers. "I'm surprised they are blooming this time of year."

"Primrose are cold weather flowers, they only bloom in winter."

"Very romantic." Blue whispered.

"Yes, it is."

"You know what else is romantic?"

She looked at him curiously.

Blue hugged her, "I got us a room next door for tonight."

"Really?"

"Yes, an actual bed and a hot shower."

Eryn stood on her toes and kissed him on the cheek. "Thank you."

"Wanna have an early dinner?"

She had the sense that Blue was up to something, but she wasn't sure what, "Did you have anything in mind?"

"Well, are you in the mood for anything special? Steak dinner, tacos, Italian?"

"Hmm, all good options, I'm in the mood for manicotti, what about you?"

"The lady wants manicotti; she will have manicotti." He took her hand and led her inside to get directions to the best Italian restaurant in town.

On the way back to the Inn, it started to snow just a little. A few late winter flurries and Blue pulled Eryn under a streetlight.

"Blue, isn't this perfect?"

"Not quite."

"What? How can you say this isn't...."

Blue took both of her hands and sunk to one knee, Eryn Elizabeth Upton, will you do me the honor of being my wife?" As he spoke the words, he slipped a hand into his pocket and presented Eryn with the ring he had purchased earlier.

Eryn stared down at him, her mouth as open in shock and she wasn't sure she heard him correctly, but she must have because he was kneeling in front of her holding a ring. The most beautiful ring she had ever seen.

"Yes."

"Yes?" Blue couldn't believe his ears. He stood up and slipped the ring on her finger and kissed her deeply.

Eryn felt like she was dreaming and any moment she was going to wake up and find herself asleep on her desk at work or something. Blue held her hand all the way back to the Inn and carried her up the stairs.

Once her coat was off in the room Eryn started to shiver.

"Are you cold? Did you catch a chill out walking today?" Blues face was a mask of concern. "Here I'll run you a hot shower to warm you up."

Eryn was tempted to tell him that she wasn't shivering from the cold but wanted a moment alone that the shower would afford her to let it sink in that she just agreed to marry Blue after only knowing him a couple of months. She looked down at the fairytale ring he had bought for her she didn't even want to think about how much it must have cost.

"Thank you," she said as she closed the bathroom door and stripped as the steam from the shower filled the tiny bathroom. The warm spray help to calm her nerves and she found that while the prospect of being married terrified her she had never been happier in her life. She wondered if she should text Penn and tell her to change the theme of the party, but then decided to surprise her instead the look on Penn's face would be priceless.

Their love making that night was magical and she didn't care if they never returned to Gates Point.

Chapter Eighteen

When Eryn and Blue returned to the marina in Gates Point, she found she didn't want to leave the boat. She had driven herself there so it wasn't like she could even invite Blue in for a drink when she got home. Leaving him like this was much harder than she ever imagined. But, after the boat had been unloaded and secured there wasn't much left to do but to say goodbye. But she knew he needed to get ready for work tomorrow.

She stood on the dock holding his hand. "I can't imagine what life is going to be like now."

"What do you mean?"

"I mean, I don't want to say goodbye, I don't want us to have to go back to work and not be able to talk all day or not even see you for twenty-four hours."

He grinned at her, his eyes warm, his touch gentle as he hugged her. "I feel the same way."

"We both have to work; this is just terrible." She felt him chuckle while he continued to hold her. "We can talk later this evening after we both check in."

"Okay," she pulled back from him. He refused to let her pull too far away. He bent down and kissed her.

"Besides, I'm sure Penn and Sarah have missed you."

"I guess." He had a point she couldn't wait to show them the ring.

He kissed the top of her head and released her. "I'll call you later."

Eryn drove home a mix of emotions; she couldn't wait to call Penn and she was already missing Blue. She unpacked her clothes and sorted them to be washed every time her ring caught the light she stopped and stared at it. It was beautiful and perfect. She went to the kitchen next in search of something to eat. She needed to go the store, then she decided to call Penn and Sarah and invite them over for dinner.

She sent a group text.

"Ladies I am home and starving, do you want to pick up some takeout and come to my place so I can fill you in on my week?"

"On our way," Penn responded, "Sarah you stop for beer, I'll get the food."

"Deal" Sarah answered.

Eryn smiled and waited. She took off her ring and slipped it into her jeans pocket.

Sarah arrived first, "I'm so glad your home!" She declared hugging Eryn.

"Were there problems with the nursery?"

"Not at all, but it is just so much to deal with, I can't believe you left me in charge!"

"Well, sounds like I made the right decision." Eryn hugged Sarah back.

Penn came bursting in, "Hello!"

"Here let us help you." Eryn reached for one of the bags Penn was carrying.

"Thank you, I got some of everything. I hope you like it."

The three ladies headed for the kitchen.

"How was your trip?" Penn asked suggestively.

"It was wonderfu,l of course. It was cold naturally but very beautiful."

"Really, I'm surprised you saw any of it!"

"Penn!" Sarah fussed.

Eryn stopped unpacking food "Well, listen there is something I want to tell you." She slid her hand into her pocket.

"Oh?" Penn paused to look at her.

Eryn took the ring out of her pocket and slipped it back on her finger and then held up her left hand.

Penn and Sarah screamed at the same time. Penn reached out and grabbed her hand, "Let me see that!"

"Holy hell! That is gorgeous!" Sarah exclaimed.

The two friends hugged Eryn.

"I have to admit I'm impressed with Blue's taste in jewelry."

Eryn looked down at it. "It is beautiful, isn't it?"

Penn returned to organizing the food. "Okay let's get this dished out and sit down and then you," She pointed a finger at Eryn," are going to tell us everything."

After Eryn had shared nearly every single detail about the proposal and the trip. Penn sat back and looked thoughtful, "Well now we have to change the party."

"What? Why?" Sarah and Eryn asked.

"Well not it needs to be an engagement party."

Eryn shot her a look, "No it absolutely does not to need to be an engagement party. If you turn it in to one, I'm not going."

"You have to go; it would be in your honor!" Penn pouted.

"And Blue wouldn't go either. We don't want a big fuss over this, save it for the wedding."

Penn narrowed her gaze, "I'm going to hold you to that, Eryn!"

"Fine."

"Great, have you set a date yet?"

"No Penn, I haven't" Eryn rolled her eyes.

"Perfect, that gives us plenty of time to plan."

Sarah laughed, "This is going to be fun!"

"I think I'll elope!"

"No, you won't, young lady. I will hog tie you and drag you to the alter if I have to!"

Eryn threw her fortune cookie at Penn. "I think I can take you."

"Ha!"

The three of them sat laughing, each thinking how wonderful their lives were in that moment.

The End

Chapter Eleven

B lue woke up at his usual time. He felt like he had been run over by a truck. He knew it wasn't the beer from the previous night but his emotional and physical state.

He showered and dressed and went downstairs to make coffee to find Chuck asleep on the sofa.

"What are you doing here?"

"Uh?" Chuck opened one eye and stared up at Blue. "Oh, I was keeping an eye on things down here in case there was any more kidnapping attempts."

"I see, that." Blue chuckled. "Want some coffee?"

"Sure."

"What are you going to do?" Chuck asked.

"Everything I can. Hopefully, the computer squad found out something useful that will give us a lead."

"Any more thoughts on possible suspects."

"No, not really."

"Well, hang in there, something will break. Give me a call if you need anything." Chuck stood to leave.

"Thanks."

Sarah spent the morning talking to the employees and helping Ryan make sure deliveries were on schedule. The retail shop was a little slow and by lunch time Sarah was ready to sit down and try to relax for a minute. She pulled out her phone and as a distraction logged into her social media account. She immediately got a message.

"You haven't been on in a while, everything okay?" A person whose name she didn't recognize as someone she knew by meeting them in person asked.

"Not really. My boss is in trouble, and I have no way to help her."

"Is she a good boss?"

"Oh yeah the best!"

"What kind of trouble?"

"Not sure, she is missing. And I'm heartbroken she is so sweet and kind. Not just to me but everyone."

"I'm sure it will work out. Do you have a friend you can call for support?"

"Yeah, sort of. I mean I just started working here not that long ago and my boss was my real friend here."

"What about a boyfriend or something?"

"No boyfriend."

"Oh."

"Ex-boyfriend."

"Not that I can call."

"That's too bad."

"Well, I'm here if you need to talk."

"Thanks."

Sarah signed out and got back to work. Something about the person was on the edge of her mind. Was it possible to get a vibe from social media? She wasn't sure but if so, she was definitely getting one. A weird one.

She went home exhausted she hadn't heard from the police, and she didn't know that they would call her anyway. But she had hoped that Blue would call even if it was unofficial.

She dialed Penn's number.

"Penn? It's Sarah."

"Hey, how are you holding up?"

"I don't know, I felt kind of numb at work today. Have you heard anything?"

"No."

"Nothing from Blue?"

"No."

Sarah sighed. "This is horrible. I don't know if I can do this."

"Why don't you come over."

"No, thank you. I think I am just going to get into my PJs and curl up with a movie and cry."

"I get it. Call if you want to talk."

"You, too." Sarah smiled at the phone. Penn was turning out to be a really good friend. She could see what Eryn liked her.

The two women clicked off.

Sarah went to her computer hoping for another distraction.

A few more of her friends were online, unfortunately most of them moved away from Gates Point, like Amy who was now living in Florida. And Jo in California.

A private message popped up in the corner of her screen, it was the same girl from earlier in the day.

"Hey, how are you feeling?"

"Terrible."

"Still upset about your boss?"

"Yeah."

"I'm sorry."

"What are you going to do if she doesn't come back?"

"Don't say things like that!"

"Sorry, just being realistic."

"Right now, I need hope, not negative thoughts."

"Okay, sorry." The girl named Emily continued, "you said earlier you don't have a boyfriend is that right?"

Sarah was getting that weird vibe again. "Yeah, that's right, why?"

"Me either."

"I was just thinking, it's too bad you have to work at all."

"What do you mean?"

"I mean if you had a boyfriend or were married you wouldn't have to work at all."

"Why wouldn't I work if I was married?"

"Because your husband would work and take care of you, and you could take care of the children and the house."

"What if I don't want children?" Sarah was getting really annoyed.

"Why wouldn't you want children?!"

"Because, they cost a lot of money, they take a lot of time and if you're not able or willing to put in the time they turn out to be selfish monsters."

"Wow, that is harsh."

"Maybe, I will feel different but right now I don't want children. Like I said that isn't really something I think about since I am not in a meaningful relationship anyway."

She hoped she sounded as snippy as she felt. Who was this person anyway?

"You just need the right man."

"I don't need a man at all!!!!"

"Not even your ex-boyfriend?"

"Especially, my ex-boyfriend."

"You sound a little hostile."

"I don't care, my friend is missing, and you are badgering me about getting married and having children. Where do I know you from anyway?"

The girl signed off without further comment.

Now Sarah was furious, how dare this person presume to tell her how to live her life especially with her antiquated ideas.

She hadn't been hungry all day, but now that she was awake, and her anger had her blood pumping she decided she was hungry. She went to the kitchen in search of anything easy and fattening. She wasn't going to worry about calories at a time like this.

She turned on a movie and ate her dinner of a fried pork chop and instant mashed potatoes. The movie was an older one, but it was about a guy using computers and cameras to spy on his tenants in the apartment building. She started thinking about the girl online again and logged back in and checked the girl's profile.

There wasn't a lot of information there. She claimed to be from Gates Point with a degree from Old Dominion University in Computer Science. Sarah thought about it. Why would a girl who went to the effort of getting a degree in a very technical program be in favor of being a stay at home mom. Something wasn't adding up in her mind. She tried searching other social media sites for the girl, including ODU alumni groups and professional networking sites. Nothing. She was starting to get a really bad feeling about this woman online. She clicked off and called Blue.

"Blue, it's Sarah. I'm sorry to call so late."

"That's okay, I'm at the office, what's up?"

"I had a weird experience today and I'm not sure if he has anything to do with Eryn's disappearance, but I have a weird feeling that it might."

"What happened?"

"I was online and a woman who friended me a few days ago that I have never met in person sent me a private message and she was saying some pretty weird things like, I shouldn't be working for Eryn and stuff." Sarah felt like crying, "It sounds stupid when I say it out loud but it gave me such a creepy feeling like this person was judging Eryn."

Blue sat up straight in his chair.

"Do you know the screen name of this person?"

"Yes,"

"Can you give me the screen name and which social site you were using?"

"Sure."

Sarah pulled up the site to double check the name and then read everything on the profile to Blue."

"Okay Sarah. I want you to try and get some rest. I am going to have someone in our computer forensics division get started on this, I'll call you in the morning and let you know what we have found."

"Okay, thanks. I hope this isn't something stupid and I am just being paranoid."

"Every lead helps, I'm glad you called."

"Good night."

"Good night, Sarah."

Blue clicked off. He got up and took the elevator down to the sixth floor.

He pushed the door open to the computer lab as they called it.

The lights were dim as most of the department was gone for the night.

He heard the clicking of computer keys in the corner and a lone desk lamp on.

He walked to the far corner of the room. A young man with headphones was sitting in a cubicle bobbing his head to music only he could hear and typing furiously in what Blue knew was computer code but had no idea what any of it meant.

"Excuse me." He said loud enough to be heard over the music.

The young man jumped and pulled off the headphones.

"Oh my god, you scared the hell out of me!"

He did seem breathless Blue noticed.

"Sorry, didn't mean to."

The young man looked him over and realization dawned on his face. "Uh sorry, Chief. How can I help you?"

"Are you a detective?"

"No sir, just a technician."

"Can you help me with an online profile. It might be case of harassment, and it might help us find a kidnap victim."

"Whoa! Yeah, I can help with that."

"Okay, good." Blue looked around and pulled over a wheeled desk chair and sat down next to the young man.

"What's your name?"

"Ted, sir."

"Well, Ted we have a real problem. We have a woman who vanished only her coffee and keys were found at the scene along with her car. Someone disabled the alarm system remotely and seems to be hiding their tracks pretty well."

"But?"

"But tonight, a friend of the missing woman was online and started receiving strange private messages from someone she doesn't know. We think the two things might be connected."

"Do you have the site and the screen name of both the person being harassed and the person doing the harassing?"

"I have the screen name of the person who is harassing the friend. I don't have the friends screen name. But I can get it."

"Let me see if I need it first."

Ted looked at the information Blue and scribbled on a piece of paper and typed.

He entered the social media site for friends online and searched the screen name and given name of the person on the paper.

"Okay, found the harasser."

"Interesting. They are only friends with one person online."

"Is that unusual?"

Blue who did not have a social media account or any desire for one wasn't up to date with online culture.

"Very, the point of friends online is to connect with everyone you've ever known, friends from school, people you met at a party who might be fun or interesting. People you work with, most people have hundreds of friends they are connected with online."

"Really?"

"Yeah. It is a big red flag when a person is only friends with a handful of other people."

"What if they are new to the site."

"That's possible. But they would have posted things like places they've been, movies they'd seen or something to help connect with their friends. This person has none of that. Another red flag is if someone is following a bunch of people who haven't friended them back and has very few posts."

"What does that mean?"

"It is usually guys trolling for dates, it's also a way for pedophiles to meet victims and human traffickers to find people that are easy targets."

Blue knew of course about the cybercrimes divisions cases, but he never thought about how it all worked.

"So, for our current victim of this harassment to accept a friendship from this person with so few posts or other friends is pretty dangerous."

"Is there any way for you to see what this person said to our victim?"

"I either need the screen name of the other person, since the messages were sent privately or a warrant."

Blue was glad this young man was aware and obeyed the law and policies of the department.

"Hang on."

He took out his cell phone and called Sarah back.

"Sarah, it's Blue."

"Did you find anything?"

"We're still working on it, listen to get the private messages I either need your screen name or a warrant and frankly I don't want to wait until morning to try and get a warrant."

"No problem I'll give it to you."

"Listen, I'm going to put you on speaker, I'm here with one our computer technicians, his name is Ted. Are you okay with giving him the information?"

"I guess so." Sarah was hesitant.

"Listen Sarah, I understand your reluctance but, I promise you that Ted is a good guy, and you won't be harassed by him after this is over. Because he works in my building and he knows I carry a really big gun, don't you Ted?"

"Yes, chief." Ted's voice was a little shaky.

Sarah could imagine Blue tower over some poor computer geek.

"Blue, don't scare him. If you trust him then I trust him."

"Thank you, Sarah."

"Hi, Ted."

"Hi."

"My screen name is bookishgirl."

"And your password."

Sarah hesitated.

"Sarah if you are uncomfortable, we can come to you."

"No, no. That won't be necessary."

Sarah gave Ted her password. She heard him clicking away on the keyboard.

"Just change the password after we hang up." Ted advised.

"Okay."

"Okay, I am logging into your messages. I'm only looking at the ones you received from the person named Emily."

"Okay." Sarah agreed.

It only took Ted a few minutes to find the messages and download them.

"Okay Sarah, I've downloaded them all, so I am going to log out of your account. You can change your password now if you want to." Ted informed her.

"Okay."

"Sarah, it's Blue, listen don't change the way you operate on social media, just act like you normally do, it may help us catch this guy."

"If you think it will help."

"Yes, don't let on that you suspect that Emily is anything other than what she claims to be, just make sure you download and save the messages and send them to Ted, can you do that?"

"Sure."

Ted gave her his email address and they ended the call.

Sarah sat staring at her computer screen for a moment and then logged in. She didn't change her password right away in case Ted needed it again. She would change it when all of this was over. She surfed around to see if Emily had posted anything that might be a clue.

There were no posts on Emily's page, but a message popped up.

"Hey, I thought you might be online, everything okay?"

"Yeah, my friend is still missing so I'm having to do some of her duties and mine at work."

She tried to stay neutral but also wanted to get this Emily talking. Her hands were shaking because she was worried that Blue might be right, and Emily was really Rob. Her imagination also started to wonder what if it wasn't Rob, and it was some other kind of online stalker. She wanted to log off, she wanted to close down her social media account altogether. But she knew she couldn't not if it would help find Eryn.

"That stinks."

"Yeah, I like her an all, but it is really hard right now. I am beginning to think, I wish I didn't have to work at all."

"Really? What would you do?"

"I'm not sure, I mean you're going to think this sounds silly, but I'm beginning to understand the homeschooling, stay at home mom thing you mentioned earlier. I never thought I would but lately I've been wondering if I was too quick to judge."

Sarah remembered Rob saying something about having a family one day. She hoped this helped.

About The Author

Lynn is a native of the Hampton Roads region of Virginia, the area which is the inspiration for the Gates Point series. She enjoys time in, on and around the Chesapeake Bay and its tributaries. When she isn't out exploring, she enjoys spending time at home with her husband in the garden.

Sign up for updates on new releases and behind the scenes inspirations for the Gates Point series. Visit www.stitchesandstories.com

If you enjoyed this book, please help others find it by leaving a review. Thank you.